MW01633335

SEARCHING FOR SOPHIA (SPECIAL FORCES: OPERATION ALPHA)

MOUNTAIN RESCUE
BOOK ONE

JULIA BRIGHT

This book is a work of fiction. Names, characters, places, and incidents are products of the author's imagination or used fictitiously. Any resemblance to actual events or locales or persons living or dead is entirely coincidental.

© 2023 ACES PRESS, LLC. ALL RIGHTS RESERVED

No part of this work may be used, stored, reproduced or transmitted without written permission from the publisher except for brief quotations for review purposes as permitted by law.
This book is licensed for your personal enjoyment only. This book may not be re-sold or given away to other people. If you would like to share this book with another person, please purchase an additional copy for each recipient. If you're reading this book and did not purchase it, or it was not purchased for your use only, please purchase your own copy.

Dear Readers,

Welcome to the Special Forces: Operation Alpha Fan-Fiction world!

If you are new to this amazing world, in a nutshell the author wrote a story using one or more of my characters in it. Sometimes that character has a major role in the story, and other times they are only mentioned briefly. This is perfectly legal and allowable because they are going through Aces Press to publish the story.

This book is entirely the work of the author who wrote it. While I might have assisted with brainstorming and other ideas about which of my characters to use, I didn't have any part in the process or writing or editing the story.

I'm proud and excited that so many authors loved my characters enough that they wanted to write them into their own story. Thank you for supporting them, and me!

READ ON!
Xoxo
Susan Stoker

Sophia dropped her bag on the table in the middle of the coffee shop and plopped down in a straight-back chair with the thin seat pad facing the door. Since escaping her old life and being able to make decisions on her own, she hated having her back to anyone. A nervous glance to the tables along the back wall of the shop assured her he wasn't here.

She needed to make sure he wasn't sneaking up on her. Not that he had any idea where she was now, but still the sliver of fear kept her on edge.

A shiver snaked through her right as her phone pinged. She pulled it out, frowning at the text begging her to return home. It was still early in the day and the threats hadn't started coming in. A memory of being on the ground, him swinging the broom stick, breaking it as it hit her arm slid through her and she pushed it away. He would ruin her life if she didn't cut him out.

"New in town?" The voice interrupted Sophia, and she turned to shoot daggers at the man who'd interrupted her but was met with a bald, grandfatherly-looking man with wide eyes. His smile spread slowly as he took her in. He looked harmless as a kitten, and she couldn't bring herself to tell him to mind his business.

"Sorry." She blew out a breath and shook her head, trying to push away the worry inside. "I'm just visiting."

"Are you running from something or to it?"

His question made her look at him deeper. Why would he ask that? What did he know? Had Brandon planted someone here? Had he known where she would show up? She'd turned off location services on her phone and searched for tracking applications but hadn't found any.

"No." She sounded defensive. "I'm not running."

"Silas, give the woman a break," a deep male voice cut into their conversation.

She turned to the door, surprised to see a newcomer standing in front of her table. He looked to be about her age—scratch that, he was a few years older than her and tall. How had he entered the cafe without making a noise?

"I'm not bothering her. I'm just worried because she came inside in such a huff."

She couldn't take the scrutiny. No one could know she'd ended up here in Fallport. She'd picked this town because it was off the beaten path and tucked far enough away from the interstate that someone looking for her wouldn't necessarily find her. But she didn't need a nosy old man jumping into her business.

She picked up her bag and was about to leave when the sweet scent of cinnamon hit, and her stomach rumbled so loudly that both Silas and the new stranger heard it.

"You're hungry. Stay and have a cup of coffee and one of those cinnamon rolls," tall, dark, and handsome said before he walked over to the counter to place an order. "I'll be back in a minute."

"That's Daniel." Silas' eyes flashed with something akin to excitement. "He's one of those you don't want to annoy."

Sophia turned to stare at Daniel as he placed his order. He was tall, six-three, maybe six-four, with a broad chest and trim waist, and looked fit. He had dark hair, a beard, and long fingers that had no trouble twirling his phone before he dropped it into a holder on his belt. He looked like a man who knew how to do things and knew he could do them. There wasn't the fragility she'd come to recognize in Brandon and his friends or her brother. Daniel knew his worth.

Her stomach rumbled again, reminding her she really was hungry. She'd stopped eating anything other than found food after the first week when she couldn't find a job. She'd rather starve herself than use a credit card. She had some cash zipped away in her jacket, but that had to last. It wasn't much anyway, and she would need a job soon. But employers asked questions and wanted her information, which she couldn't give. Character references were out, too, not that anyone back home would give her any praise. They all thought she'd taken advantage of Brandon when it really was the other way around.

"Here you go."

Daniel set two coffee cups on the table, one closer to her and the other near the empty chair. He also placed a sandwich and one of those amazing-smelling cinnamon rolls in front of her. She glanced up and then back at the food.

"I can't pay you back."

He nodded. "Think of it as a welcome gift."

Her stomach twisted as she stared at the food and then back up at him. She was about to tell him it was too much when Silas put in his two cents.

"You can pay him back in other ways." The cackle from Silas as he stood and walked out of the restaurant made her want to hide.

Shock filled her, along with embarrassment. She couldn't believe the old man had said that loudly in this crowded coffee shop. Her gaze landed on Daniel, and her face felt like she'd spent all weekend baking in the sun. She was sure it probably looked like it, too.

Daniel shook his head and rolled his eyes. "Sorry about that. You don't have to pay me back. He can be rude."

"I-I…I don't know what to say."

"Why don't you start with your name?"

She picked up the coffee and sipped it because she didn't know what else to do. She'd thought about giving a fake name but didn't want to mess up and not answer when speaking to someone. Her real name was Angela Sophie McDonald, so she went with Sophia Smith. That would be easy to remember.

"Sophia."

Daniel smiled, the corners of his eyes crinkling just a little. Her gaze slid over his features, taking in his brown eyes that were full of light, not muddy with anger like Brandon's had been. His skin looked kissed from the sun, but healthy. His broad shoulders bulged with muscles that made her think he did physical labor for his job. But this guy wasn't intimidating, not like the men from her past. She didn't sense the raw aggression close to the surface.

The whole picture made her think the mountain man look with the thick dark beard was a recent addition. He seemed confident, but kind. He caught her off guard. She believed he didn't want to hurt her, which thinking like that, giving him the benefit of doubt, might be a huge mistake.

The door opened, and a group of young girls, probably fifteen, came in with their phones out like they were filming or taking photographs. Panic hit hard and she ducked her head and pulled out a ball cap, placing it so the bill covered her face.

The girls were loud, interrupting more than just the two of them as they ordered their sweet coffees and muffins. They were inside the shop all of five minutes, but it felt like a lifetime as they laughed and took selfies, talking about posting to social media.

Daniel had moved his chair closer, blocking the

line of sight to the counter where the girls were standing. Once they left, she breathed out a sigh of relief. She didn't know how to explain her reaction, but Daniel didn't seem to need an explanation.

"Where are you staying while you're here?"

Daniel's question made her gaze swing to him. Why was he asking? The panic ebbed as she saw the caring look in his gaze. Could she trust him?

She didn't have a place to stay or money to stay at a hotel. The last place she'd spent any time at was a state park. She'd hoped the food would have been more plentiful, but most of the campers had eaten everything they'd brought with them. The one good thing that had come from the side trip had been a tent. She'd rescued the small tent from a couple who'd talked about tossing it after their vacation was over.

There was no way this guy with the caring brown eyes would think she could rough it in a tent, but she'd been roughing it halfway across the United States. In Texas she'd slept under overpasses, in Louisiana she'd found parks, in Mississippi and Tennessee she'd slept in old warehouses and dilapidated buildings. She hadn't spent long in Kentucky, but she'd stayed in barns and old buildings, then found the tent.

She flashed a smile, trying to put him at ease. "The hotel."

"Ah. If it's not to your standards, Whitney Crawford runs Chestnut Street Manor. She serves a mean breakfast and allows her guest access to her refrigerator."

She nodded, knowing she wouldn't have enough money to stay at a nice B&B. "Thank you."

Maybe this wasn't the town for her. It was out of the way, and the coffee shop was nice, but she worried she wouldn't find a place to work. Maybe she should ask this guy if he knew anywhere hiring who paid in cash.

When she glanced back at him, he was studying her. Then his expression went blank, and he stood.

"I need to get to work. If you want, you can stop by the nursery on the edge of town out by the RV park off Main Street—that's this street. Go out the door and go to the left."

She nodded and flashed a smile, knowing she wouldn't end up at the nursery. Trusting anyone would be a mistake, even men who drew her in with their kindness and warm smiles.

Daniel stepped outside and she watched him walk over to a brown truck with writing on the side. She narrowed her gaze, making out the word Nursery. She sighed, wishing her life had turned out different. The food and coffee helped not only with her hunger, but life didn't seem so depressing. She still needed to figure out what to do, but she could stay close for a few nights, camp in the forest, and then head out once she felt she'd worn out her welcome.

The chill of the morning disappeared, and she hiked into the forest, making sure to mark her trail by breaking a low branch that no one would notice. She'd learned how to navigate trails when she'd been younger before her father passed away. Back then, she didn't think anything would ever be bad.

Now she knew life had a way of reaching in and squishing your guts until you gave up. She was almost at that point again. Whatever strength she'd gained that allowed her to run was almost all used up. Living this way was difficult. It had been two weeks since she'd had a hot meal, and this morning's sandwich and muffin with the coffee had almost been too much. Just the thought of going back in the morning and grabbing another sandwich and a deli-cious treat made her mouth water.

She slashed her hand in front of her, trying to physically push away the thought. No way could she even consider getting another sandwich for free. She hadn't wandered too far from the town that she couldn't go back and find a good bit of trash from a dumpster or park.

People threw perfectly good food away. She'd been one of those people not too long ago. Then Brandon happened. Luckily, she hadn't given up everything when he'd asked her to. She'd given in to his demands and moved into his place. Then he promised to take care of her if she quit her job. He'd wanted her to close her bank account, but she'd put him off, not wanting to give up her money. He tried to get her to change her cellphone plan, but she'd lied and said she couldn't. That lie had made her feel like a failure at the time.

The memory of coming to after that awful night made her queasy. He'd come home early and found her dancing in the bathroom as she scrubbed the sink and tub and cleaned up the place. She'd only been wearing her bra and panties, and he'd accused her of cheating. She had no idea where he'd gotten that idea, but he'd been pissed and taken it out on her.

The memory brought up a load of pain and she unconsciously rubbed her wrists. He'd tied her up and left her in the shower after dousing her with water. Before Brandon had headed out for the rest of the evening, he'd turned the air conditioner to high and positioned a fan to blow on her. She'd thought she would freeze to death. By the time Brandon came home and freed her, she almost couldn't feel her fingers. But the night hadn't gotten any better for her. In fact, it had been much, much worse.

So what if she had to eat from a trash can? She was free. Free to think as she liked and do as she liked. She could go anywhere she wanted. The wounds on her wrists had healed, and the scars had faded, but she never forgot what Brandon had done. She would survive, if only out of spite.

Her phone buzzed, and she jumped. She usually turned it off unless she had plans to charge it. She pulled it out and read the message on the screen.

BRANDON: You can't hide. I know where you are.

PANIC FLASHED HOT. If he knew where she was, she would be dead. Dark had already fallen, and she didn't dare hike back to the town at night. She would have to wait until morning to flee.

CHAPTER TWO

Daniel Whelan checked the soil for the saplings in the mid-sized containers. He needed to get some water on these tomorrow if it didn't rain. He pulled up the weather application on his phone and noticed that snow was a possibility at the end of the week. He grunted as he shoved his phone into his pocket.

"Hey, Whelan, what are you grunting about?" Ethan asked.

Daniel turned and flashed a smile at the former SEAL who he'd met back in the Navy. This man was one of the reasons he'd moved here to Fallport.

"Snow."

"Oh yeah, I saw that on the radar. I guess our gorgeous fall weather will turn sooner than any of us hoped for."

"Right. So what brings you in?"

"I'm looking for some flowers. Just something Lilly can put into colorful pots as the winter enters the picture."

Daniel nodded, thinking about which plants would do well. "I have some that were delivered yesterday. I don't think they've all been picked through. Let's go up front, and I'll show you what we have and which ones are more likely to live through this first cold spell."

"Thanks, man."

He helped Ethan find some flowers and was helping load them when he glanced across the street and spied the young woman he'd bought the sandwich for. It had been a few days, and he hadn't seen her. He'd been wondering if she was still around. Her lips were pressed together, and her eyes narrowed as she stared at her phone screen. He saw her mutter something and then shake her head.

"You know her?" Ethan asked.

He shook his head. "Not really. Ran into her at the coffee shop. She looked like she'd been living rough, with dirty nails and hair. She didn't have the best smell about her. I bought her coffee and a sandwich."

"She was camping up by the boulders. I saw her while I was out hiking. I don't think she saw me."

Daniel should stay out of her business, but something had drawn him to her, and it wasn't just that he felt sorry for her. That was a huge part, but she had something about her that made him want to know more. "So she didn't get a hotel room."

Ethan shrugged. "I'm guessing not. Thanks for helping with the flowers. I'm sure Lilly will love them."

"Give her my best. You should come for dinner soon."

"You bet."

Daniel watched as Ethan drove away. He should go back into the nursery office and start planning for the snow at the end of the week. He didn't have to do much, but he would have to move a few of the more delicate items into one of the greenhouses on the property. But that could wait.

He moved to the road and started across just as Sophia glanced up. Panic flashed on her face. Why was she here if she wasn't out here to see him?

"Everything okay?" Daniel asked as he walked faster, noticing a car had just turned onto the road not too far away.

Sophia shook her head and looked like she might

run. But the car was there, keeping her in place. "I-I didn't realize this was where you worked. I'm fine. I didn't see the nursery." She slapped her palm against her forehead. "I'm just—never mind. I wasn't paying attention. I don't need anything. I'm going to go."

Her hands were shaking, and her gaze darted to her phone more than four times in the short few seconds he'd been talking to her. Her fingernails still had dirt in the nail beds, and her hair looked like it hadn't been washed in a few days.

Her phone buzzed, and she jumped. Panic didn't just flash across her features. It consumed her. He reached out and placed his hand on her shoulder.

"Hey, come inside and get some tea. I was just about to have some. I need a break. I have a washing machine in the back and a shower, too. You can take a break for a bit, and then we can talk."

She glanced at her phone, then back at him. It took a moment, but she finally nodded. He had no clue what upset her, but he didn't like seeing her so worried.

"Come on in. It's not raining yet, but I hope it will soon."

Sophia grunted but followed him. He showed her the shower and the washer.

"The dryer may take two times through. It's not

the best. I have some clothes left over from previous workers."

She turned and narrowed her gaze. "Why do you have a shower here?"

"The previous owner lived here. I have a place in town. I turned their house into my office. It's convenient when we have very dirty work. It allows us to get muddy while we work, then change our clothes before we start seeing customers. The leftover clothes are from people who used to work here and just decided to leave their old t-shirts and pants for the next worker who needed them."

"Oh," Sophia said, then turned and stepped into the bathroom, locking the door.

Daniel took care of some paperwork before he heated the water for tea. He checked the freezer, finding a frozen burrito and an egg sandwich. He would heat both and eat whichever food she didn't want. If she wanted both, he would just wait until he got home to eat.

After a moment, the shower stopped, and he moved to the kitchen to heat up the water. He was closer to the bathroom and couldn't help but hear her talking to someone. He shouldn't be listening, but that didn't stop him from straining to hear her words.

"Stop calling me."

He closed his eyes and concentrated. Listening was wrong, but he didn't move away.

"No, I'm not telling you where I am."

Sophia's words were crisp. He had hoped she would feel better after her shower, but maybe that wasn't in the cards for her.

The microwave dinged just as she opened the bathroom door. He turned, seeing her shock as she stepped out into the hall.

"Were you listening?"

Daniel moved closer and held up his hands. "I wasn't trying to."

"I should go," Sophia snapped.

"No, wait. Please don't go."

Sophia's shoulders heaved as she breathed. Her gaze shot to the microwave where the hot burrito sat, making the room smell like delicious Mexican food. Conflict flashed in her eyes. Her stomach rumbled, but he wasn't sure she would stick around. He had to find a way to convince her to stay. Even if it was only long enough for her to eat the burrito.

CHAPTER THREE

Her brother, Kyle, wasn't on her side. He was a lot like Brandon. Arrogant, rude, and controlling, but he'd never laid a hand on her. She still couldn't trust him to keep her location a secret. Maybe it was time to change her phone number and cut off all communication with her past.

"Listen, I know you're hungry."

Hot anger swirled around her belly. "Don't listen in on my conversations. Got that?"

He lifted his hands in surrender again. "Okay. Got it. I won't listen."

The scent coming from the kitchen was about to do her in. The last fresh, hot meal she'd eaten had been when she'd first arrived in this town, and

Daniel had given it to her. Her gaze strayed to the counter, but she couldn't see any food sitting out.

"What did you cook?"

Daniel glanced over his shoulder and then met her gaze again. She thought his eyes made him look nice. She regretted yelling at him. The thought of him—anyone—knowing what was going on in her life made her squirm. Nice people didn't have to run and hide from their boyfriends—fiancé. Did he still count as a fiancé? She'd tried to end it so many times, and each time she'd found herself chained to the floor or locked in his basement. The title of fiancé and the expectation to marry him had existed between them, but her will to marry Brandon had fled long before she had.

"A local woman makes the burritos and sells them. They're delicious. Homemade, not store-bought. This is from last week, though I've kept it frozen, so it's still good."

Anticipation wound through her. She wanted to eat whatever Daniel placed in front of her. She took a step toward the kitchen and then froze. What if he wasn't going to let her eat it? What if it was for him? A special burrito made by a local woman wasn't something people shared. Her gaze flashed to his again, and he smiled. Again with the kind eyes. He looked so nice it made her stomach ache.

"It smells great." She prayed he wouldn't keep the food from her. That had to have been one of Brandon's cruelest tactics. Forcing her to starve. He'd thought it would make her love him. It hadn't.

Daniel backed up, and she stepped past him and into the kitchen. He pulled the food from the microwave and placed it on the table. She pounced on the food, taking the first bite with her head bent over the plate, her arms sticking out so she could protect her food like a feral dog. She felt a bit like a feral dog, not a stray cat. Stray cats were sleek and in control. Dogs were desperate when they went feral. She took another bite before he could tell her the burrito had been for him.

She expected him to say something when he sat across from her, but he just sipped his tea like it was normal to have some stranger wolfing down food like a starving mongrel.

After she finished the burrito, she noticed he'd pushed the egg sandwich closer to her. Guilt twisted, and she thought about telling him she didn't need it, but hunger clawed at her belly. She needed the food, even if it made her look like a pig.

Her gaze hung on her wrist, noting how boney

she looked. Nothing would make her look like a pig. Anyone paying attention would notice she was close to starving.

When she'd first moved in with Brandon, she probably had twenty-five, maybe thirty pounds that she'd wanted to lose before her wedding. Back then, her concerns had been simple, immature, like an innocent child. Now she knew a wedding wouldn't fix anything, and getting married could be just as much of a prison as an actual jail.

Brandon's starvation tactics had peeled off weight. At first, she'd been thrilled, but then actual hunger had set in, making her forget tasks in the middle of doing them. There had been days he'd not allowed her anything but water. She'd grown weak.

Since leaving Brandon, the weight had fallen off as she'd hiked across the country, finding herself in their small corner of the world where a big guy, much bigger than Brandon, with kind eyes, had fed her twice with no expectations. At least, she thought there were no expectations.

She put the egg sandwich down and narrowed her gaze. "Why are you feeding me?"

He shrugged. "You looked hungry."

Worry filled her. "You don't expect anything?"

His lips tipped up, and worry enveloped her. She

sat up straighter, thinking about her shoes and how she couldn't run without them.

"If you wanted to work a little in the morning, help me move some pots into the greenhouse, you could sleep on the pull-out couch tonight. You'd be alone but have a warm bed, shower, and food." He stood up and opened the refrigerator. "There's not much food. Some eggs that are still good, stuff to make sandwiches, and coffee. Plenty of coffee. We also have cookies and chips in the pantry. It's not much."

Her stomach cramped, and tears burned her eyes. Why was he being so nice? "You'd let me stay here without me having to..." Her voice trailed off. She didn't want to finish the thought.

Daniel took a seat across from her and clasped his hands together as he leaned over, his gaze never leaving hers. "Do I find you attractive? Yes. But this is purely a friendly offer. There are no expectations other than you helping out in the morning. I need to move about fifty potted plants into the greenhouse unless a rush of people comes to buy them in the next few hours. I'll need to get those moved before the snow comes."

"Snow?" She hadn't known it was going to snow. "It's early for snow, right?"

"Yes. A cold front dipped low across the middle of the country. It's headed this way. Early snowfall. It happens, just not every year."

Her gaze fell on the sandwich as hunger and fear twisted through her. "I thought I had more time before the snow."

"Listen, do you ever clean?"

She whipped her head up and narrowed her gaze at him. "What?"

"Do you ever clean?"

She shook her head, trying to get the images of her life with Brandon out of her mind. He'd forced her to scrub the bathroom after he'd purposely taken a shit on the floor. She shivered as she deliberately pushed the memory away. "What kind of cleaning?"

He shrugged. "Some houses in town need regular cleaning, dusting, and wiping down furniture. There are a few rentals, though it's the slow time of year. The owner of the cabins needs someone to help out. She's older and wants help."

Sophia's gaze fell to the table as she took another bite of the egg sandwich. This wasn't Brandon. She wouldn't be held captive, forced to clean up a gross mess. Though it didn't sound like a lot of work, money was money. She sipped the tea, her mind whirling.

"Do they pay in cash?" She didn't want to look at him and reveal why she needed cash and not someone doing a background check on her. She couldn't let anyone from her past figure out where she was.

"I could talk to them about it. I'm sure something could be arranged."

She nibbled on the sandwich, her thoughts spinning. Could this be the solution she had been searching for? Running from Brandon hadn't gone the way she'd thought it would. Fear of being found out had pushed her from town to town, making her move even when she'd thought she'd found a good place to live for a while.

Brandon had texted her a few days ago, telling her he knew where she was, but that had been a lie. He'd sent her a photo of Mickey Mouse to indicate he thought she was in Florida. She needed to block his number, but she feared not knowing what he was thinking more than she feared having to read his mean messages. Had all of his texts with knowledge of where she'd gone just been fishing expeditions?

Maybe she hadn't needed to run when he'd texted about knowing she was in New Orleans. Could she have stayed there? And maybe she could stay here.

She took the last bite of the sandwich and washed it down with the last of the tea. When she met Daniel's gaze next, she felt better than she had in a long while.

"I can clean."

Daniel's lips twitched up. "Good. I know this place isn't the best, but you'd at least be out of the snow."

She gave her head a fast shake. "Wait, you're letting me stay here for more than just tonight?"

He nodded. "If you want. I usually show up at about six in the morning. I have a few people who work for me, and Frank comes in early one day a week so I can take time off. But the pull-out couch is in the other room, and you can lock the door."

The offer was too good to believe, but it didn't seem like Daniel was lying. His gaze stayed steady as her tears built. Finally she had to glance away. He placed a fresh napkin in front of her as he stepped out of the room and into the bathroom.

She swiped at the tears running down her cheeks, wondering if she was in a dream. After the morning she'd had, with Kyle calling, she'd thought her luck had run out. Maybe Fallport would be her saving grace, and she could stay here long enough to save some money and take a breath.

She stood and stuck her hand out. Daniel's lips twitched up into a half smile as he reached for her. His hand squeezed gently, and suddenly the relief she'd felt from taking a shower and getting clean felt real. She didn't have to run and wouldn't be caught out in the snow—if she could trust Daniel. She had to trust him. She wasn't sure, but maybe her life had just turned around.

CHAPTER FOUR

At quitting time, Daniel stepped into the office and noticed Sophia had cleaned the kitchen, wiping down the counters and washing their dishes from the snack she'd eaten earlier. He should stop by the store tonight and buy more food so she'd have something to eat.

He went in search of Sophia, finding her in the bathroom scrubbing the toilet. The sink sparkled, and the mold growing in the corner of the shower was gone.

"Wow, it looks great in here."

Sophia jerked around, the toilet brush swinging with her, almost like a weapon.

"Whoa, sorry. Didn't mean to scare you."

She glanced at the toilet brush dripping cleaning

solution on the floor and a little on his boot and grimaced.

"Sorry," she said as she turned back to the toilet to drop the brush before dropping to her knees to clean the drips from his boots.

"Hey," he reached for her shoulder but thought better of it. She seemed very jumpy, and he didn't want to make her even jumpier.

She glanced up, worry making her brown eyes appear even darker. "Sorry. I didn't know you were still here. I thought you'd already left for the day."

"I really didn't mean to scare you. I'll make sure you know I'm around next time I come in."

She shook her head, her now clean hair pulled into a ponytail moved to slap her on the face. She looked younger, maybe too young. God, he hoped she was at least eighteen. If she wasn't, someone could come after him and accuse him of stuff he would never do.

"You are over eighteen, right?"

Her lips thinned, and her eyes narrowed. "What type of question is that?"

He held up his hands, hoping to keep the peace. "I just want to make sure that whoever is after you isn't claiming you're a runaway."

Her lips thinned even more. "I'm not running away from anything."

He nodded, realizing she wasn't going to tell him anything she didn't want to. "You're safe here, Sophia."

Her shoulders sank as she blew out air, looking almost like a deflating balloon. He guessed she hadn't felt safe in a while.

"I'm heading out. Do you need anything before I go? There's stuff for sandwiches in the refrigerator. Please eat."

Her gaze didn't rise to meet his, and he felt guilty for questioning her. He turned to leave, not wanting to point out that she hadn't told him her age or who was chasing her. He'd made it to the kitchen when she stepped out of the bathroom.

"I'm twenty-two." Her voice was low, but he could still hear her.

He turned and gave her a sharp nod, not asking who was after her. She might tell him, or she wouldn't. She had to feel comfortable to tell him anything, and from what he'd seen, she was far from comfortable or secure.

"Have a good night," Daniel said as he stepped outside, making sure the place was locked up. He locked the gate after he drove out.

Sophia wasn't trapped inside since the gate was just two steel bars that crossed over the entry drive. It was there to prevent people from driving a truck onto the property and stealing a large tree or bush, not to prevent people from walking onto or off the property.

In the last year that he'd owned the place, no one had come onto the property while he was closed, except the one woman who'd been chasing her escaped dog that somehow thought the nursery would be a great place to hide. Daniel had woken the next morning and watched the security camera feed, laughing as the dog evaded capture while the owner fell in the mud. He'd felt a little bad about that, but the woman had gotten up and dusted off her clothes.

It looked like the dog thought it was a great game of chase. The woman had shown up the next day, looking incredibly sheepish as she'd explained that she'd been dog-sitting her friend's pup. She wanted to pay for any damage, but there hadn't been any. He'd become friendly with the older woman, checking in on her occasionally.

Fallport was that type of town. Friendly, with good people. He hadn't joined the search and rescue team officially, but they knew they could count on him. He enjoyed the work but couldn't get away every time they needed to go out and rescue someone who'd wandered too far off the path and couldn't find their way back.

He hadn't been here when the ghost-hunting group had come through, but he'd heard the stories. Before heading to the store, he stopped by On The Rocks for a drink and to catch up on the latest gossip.

Hank Blackburn was behind the bar. He lifted his chin as Daniel stepped up to the bar.

"You want a stout?" Hank asked.

Daniel nodded. "Yeah, a stout."

Zeke stepped out of his office and lifted his hand. "Heard you got a visitor."

Daniel rolled his eyes. "Jesus, does everyone know?"

Zeke chuckled and patted him on the back. "Well, Silas was in here earlier."

"Oh, that explains it," Daniel said, taking a sip of his beer.

"First thing in the morning, everyone in town will know," Zeke commented.

"Anything exciting in town other than my visitor?"

"Nope. All's quiet. It's good with that snow coming in. I'd hate to have to rescue someone. All the locals know what they are doing, and we don't have too many visitors right now."

"That's good."

Zeke took the seat next to Daniel. The bar wasn't too busy. As a business owner, he knew Zeke probably had a million things he could do, but sometimes breaks were needed.

"So tell me, what is up with the woman staying at your place?"

Daniel took another sip and then set his beer down. He turned to meet Zeke's gaze. "I don't know. You ever have someone you run into on a mission you could tell was in trouble and needed help? Like you knew if you didn't help them, they would be dead within the next twenty-four hours?"

Zeke nodded. "Yeah. There was this guy, maybe a kid. He was tall but skinny as a rail. I knew the moment I saw him that if I didn't help him, he would be dead by the end of the day. Of course, we were in the middle of a mission, and I couldn't do anything. Sure enough, we came back through that village the next day, and he was dead. It hurt seeing him like that. I hated myself for not helping him. But my hands were tied."

Daniel took another sip of beer. "The second I saw her the other day at Grinders, I had this feeling.

Then earlier, when she was out by the nursery, I knew if I didn't help her, she would end up dead. I don't know how I knew, but I felt it in my bones."

"So what are you going to do with her?" Zeke asked.

"I'm getting her a few cleaning jobs. I've texted a few people, and she has two cleaning jobs this week. She's helping me move the plants in tomorrow, and maybe I'll find another job for her next week. She needs money. The way she attacked the burrito I put in front of her, it was obvious she was starving."

Hank chuckled as he set a mug of beer in front of Zeke. "Sounds like you've got your hands full. Maybe she should just find her own job."

"Don't judge until you're in the same position." Zeke took a drink from the mug Hank had just placed in front of him. "You know, Whitney needs some help. I'll send her a text later."

"Thanks. I hope this woman stays around. She doesn't need to be out on her own during the winter."

Zeke nodded then glanced over his shoulder as a group of guys came in, taking Hank's attention. Zeke sipped more beer, then set his mug down and tapped the scarred wooden surface. "You think she's on the run?"

Daniel shrugged. "Maybe." He finished his beer and threw some money on the bar. "I'll find out more as she gets comfortable with everything." He turned to Zeke and lifted his eyebrows. "Do you need any help?"

Zeke shook his head. "Not now, but I'll ask around. I'm sure there's plenty of people who need a helping hand around here like Whitney."

"Thanks, Zeke. I'll see you around."

Daniel dropped by the store, not saying much to the cashier or anyone else who might just want gossip. Sophia didn't seem like the type who wanted her dirty laundry spread around town, not that he knew anything about her. Sophia might not even be her real name. Maybe he shouldn't have vouched for her, but she didn't seem like the type who would screw him over.

If she took from any of the people she was cleaning for, or if she did something egregious, he would fix it. He just hoped he hadn't been wrong about her. She seemed like the kind of person who just needed a little help. Hopefully, she wasn't plotting a way to screw him over.

CHAPTER FIVE

Sophia woke early the next morning and made sure to fold up the bed and clean the area. She'd started a load of clothes last night and tossed them into the dryer this morning. She found a pair of jeans that fit and some shoes that were in better condition than the ones she was currently wearing.

Everything about this place seemed almost too good to be true. She'd eaten a sandwich before going to bed. It was the first time in she didn't know how long that she'd gone to sleep with her belly full. She hoped this guy didn't think she was taking advantage of him. She needed this place, the safety, and comfort for a while. She should have thought about the weather before heading to West Virginia. She could have gone somewhere like Florida or the Gulf

Coast. She hadn't wanted to go to California because living costs were so expensive there. Maybe, if she could get enough work, she would be able to make a life for herself.

She pushed away the thought. Getting her hopes up wouldn't solve her problems. Doing hard work and making sure Daniel never had a reason to kick her to the curb would help more.

The door opened, and she jumped. "Oh, I didn't hear your truck."

Daniel cleaned his boots on the mat inside the door as he rubbed his hands together. "Did you sleep well?"

"Better than I have in a while."

"Are you ready to get to work?"

Sophia nodded. "I found jeans and a sweatshirt. I just need some gloves, and I'll be set."

Daniel poured himself fresh coffee she'd made up not too long ago. A twinge of guilt filled her. Maybe she shouldn't stay here. He was giving her way more than she was giving him. A place to live, even a tiny one-bedroom, was running over five hundred a month. She shouldn't stick around.

She moved to the kitchen and grabbed the mug she'd used earlier, pouring up a half cup of coffee. Sipping the coffee, she mused that this was way better than anything she'd picked up in a gas station. She'd thought about rescuing coffee cups from trash cans, but she'd found out some guys peed in their cups and then tossed them in the regular trash. The thought made her shiver.

"You okay? Too cold?" Daniel asked.

She shook her head. "No, I'm fine. It's nothing. So, what's the plan for today?"

"We'll start moving the plants into the greenhouse. Two of my employees are supposed to show up at nine, but they're on the regular schedule. Frank, one of my part-time employees, had to drive into Charlestown today."

Sophia blinked at him, unsure if she'd heard correctly. "South Carolina?"

He shook his head. "No, West Virginia. Charleston, South Carolina, is much bigger. The one here is beautiful, but I prefer Charleston, South Carolina."

"Oh, I didn't know there was one here in West Virginia."

"Did you eat breakfast?"

She didn't want to lie but felt guilty for eating his food. Then she noticed the bags he'd set down on the counter. It was more food.

"Not yet. I can get my own food, though."

"There's no need for that. You're helping out here, and I think the arrangement benefits us both."

She bit her lower lip. Maybe he wanted more than she could offer. He hadn't said he wanted sex, but she wasn't sure.

He unloaded the groceries, and she made a quick sandwich, wolfing it down so she could help him outside. She used the bathroom before they both headed out.

The wind had picked up, and clouds gathered out to the west. Daniel told her which plants needed moving, and she grabbed a cart and began taking the plants inside.

A customer showed up, and Daniel had to help them. She'd learned that his nursery was the only one in the area, so people came from all around to pick up plants and get advice on how to care for them when storms blew in.

When she was outside, near Daniel and the customer, she watched him work and listened to what he had to say. Her knowledge of plants was small, and after listening to Daniel, she guessed she knew less than nothing.

He finished with that customer, and another customer stopped by before he could get back to her. She didn't mind the work. At least she could think without someone trying to dictate what she was doing.

By the time Daniel returned to her, she'd taken all the plants inside that he'd indicated needed to go.

"I dropped into the greenhouse before coming over here. You've done a great job placing those plants. I like how you work. You know, you could get a job here."

There was no way she could work here. He would ask for her social security number, and she couldn't go on record here. If anyone found out where she was, Brandon would come after her. She'd learned a little too late her ex didn't like losing, and he wanted control over everything.

"No, thank you." She hated telling him no, and she couldn't meet his gaze. No question, she'd disappointed him. He didn't say anything or push more for her to work at his facility.

"After you clean up, would you like to go for a walk around town? We could grab burgers."

She shook her head. "You're doing too much for me. I can't pay you back."

Daniel's lips thinned, and his eyes narrowed. "I don't expect you to pay me back."

"Why are you being so nice?"

"Haven't you ever done something nice for someone? I don't expect anything from you. I just want to help."

His words made her feel like maybe her whole life had been a failure. She'd met Brandon when she'd turned seventeen, and by the time she was twenty, she had moved in with him. That had been a huge mistake. She should have dumped him at the first sign of trouble instead of clinging tighter to him. He'd gotten away with so much abuse because she believed the lie that having someone, even if that person hit her, was better than being alone.

There was no way she could stick around. Snow or not, she couldn't live with the idea of having to pay Daniel back hanging over her head. Later, she would sneak away and find a good spot in the woods to bunk down for the storm. She had survived so much already. She could weather this storm on her own.

CHAPTER SIX

Daniel wanted to say more, but Sophia seemed opposed to listening. Her expression had changed to being shut off, and her shoulders had rolled forward. He'd talk to her about it later.

They'd finished their work out here, and he sent her inside to wash up. She'd gotten much dirtier than he had because she'd done most of the work.

She'd made a sandwich in the kitchen, and instead of eating together so he could get to know her, she finished her meal alone. He wasn't angry, just disappointed she didn't want to get food together.

About an hour later, he saw her in the greenhouse, helping a customer. He waved but let her continue working, not wanting to interrupt. She answered the customer truthfully when she had no idea how to care for the plant in the coming storm.

"I'm sorry," Sophia said. "I just arrived yesterday. I'm more of a pack mule, not the brains behind the business. Hold on, and Daniel can explain everything to you."

He pretended he hadn't heard her and waited for Sophia to come over. "Do you need something?" He smiled, trying to seem as friendly as possible.

"This customer needs information on the plants she is buying."

"Sure." Daniel went over, noticing Sophia had given the woman the best-looking of the bunch. He answered the woman's questions, making sure she understood how to take care of her new plants. He suggested waiting until after the snow was gone, but she said she had guests coming and needed something pretty to liven up the beds next to the front door. He gave her the information but didn't have much hope for the plants.

"Thank you for helping," the woman said as Daniel loaded the containers into the trunk of her car.

"You're welcome."

"And that sweet girl who first helped me, thank her. She was so nice."

Daniel nodded, thinking the exact same thing. Sophia was very nice. Maybe she was too nice. The way she'd looked when she'd arrived in town told a story of a homeless person, then her skittishness showed that she was probably running from something. He could tell she had trust issues. He wanted to know more about her and why she'd come into town, dirty and hungry, with no place to stay.

Fallport was out of the way, tucked up close to the hills, a good spot to get close to the Appalachian mountains, and the main trail that covered fourteen states and was a hiker's paradise. But Sophia wasn't dressed for hiking and didn't have the gear for it. Sure, she had a thin tent that was great for casual camping, but not something that would work in the harsh environment of the Appalachian.

He wanted to know more, but Sophia wouldn't give it to him if he prodded too much. She might reveal her truths eventually, but not if he demanded.

He spent the next few hours making sure he was prepared for the storm. He'd seen Sophia around, helping out where she could. He owed her, but she didn't want to become an employee. She said she needed cash payment. She had to be running from someone and not just out here wandering around because she was bored with her life.

Close to four, after he'd double-checked the property and his inventory, he headed into the office. They'd be closing soon, and he wondered if Sophia wanted to grab some dinner. He could grab ingredients from the store, and they could cook at his place. But that seemed almost like a date. Maybe he should just say goodnight and head home.

"Sophia," Daniel called out as he entered the office. His other employees had left for the day. With the storm hitting around midnight, he'd told everyone not to bother with coming in. If the snow melted and the roads weren't bad, he'd make the call about opening in the morning.

He'd gone through half the stack of mail when he realized he hadn't heard Sophia moving in the other room.

"Sophia," he said again, this time heading to the bathroom and glancing into the laundry room. She wasn't here. "Sophia," he called louder.

He stepped outside, grabbing his coat and gloves as he left the building. "Sophia!" He moved to the greenhouse and then checked around the lot. She wasn't anywhere on the property. "Shit."

After looking in the greenhouse one more time, he headed inside and looked for her bag. It wasn't beside the pull-out couch, but he did find a note he hadn't seen earlier.

I APPRECIATE everything you've done. It was too much. I can't ever pay you back. Thank you.

SHE'D SIGNED THE NOTE, but the first letter of her name had been written as another letter, then Sophia had written over whatever she'd first started to write. Something seemed off about it all. He read the note again as anger built. There was no way she could survive this storm.

He tore out of the building, not locking the door in case she returned. First, he drove down the road to the interstate, looking for a hitchhiker, praying she wasn't stupid enough to set up her tent, thinking she could last in this weather. Sure, the storm would likely be small since it was the middle of October but being out in this storm was like going looking for trouble. Surely she'd be hurt.

After a few miles, he turned back to town and contemplated calling Zeke or one of the other guys on the search and rescue team. But he didn't know if she was out in the mountains. He didn't want to have them jump into action if she was somewhere warm.

He stopped outside the bar and closed his eyes, wishing he had an idea where she was or if she was still in town. After blowing out a frustrated breath, he headed inside, his heart heavy. He hated a few things in life, and abuse was one of them. A woman like Sophia had probably suffered abuse that sent her running. He couldn't figure out another reason why she would be here in Fallport.

Perhaps she was just flighty and out for a good time, but that didn't match anything he knew about her. He glanced around the room, and his gaze landed on a booth in the back corner. He could make out someone sitting with their elbows on the table, her long brown hair cascading to hide her face. She looked thin, and she looked similar to Sophia.

He moved closer, bypassing the bar where Hank had already set his beer. It was a little presumptuous of Hank to assume he wanted exactly what he usually ordered, but maybe he was set in his ways, and the bartender was just trying to be efficient.

When he realized the woman was Sophia, he stopped moving toward her and drew in a deep breath, counting to ten. Yelling at her would be totally wrong. She wasn't a child, and she wasn't his responsibility, but he felt responsible for her. She wasn't from here and didn't know how wicked the storms could be this early in the year. Closer to January or February, he was sure the storm would be snow, but this storm could have freezing rain, sleet, and snow. Sure, the ground was still warm, but anything could happen, and if she stayed out all night in it, she could end up freezing to death.

That last thought made him want to rush over and demand she come to her senses, but he didn't want to frighten her away. He needed to calm down and approach this as a friend.

Daniel swung back to the bar and picked up the beer. He nodded at Sophia in the back booth. "Has she eaten?"

Hank shook his head. "Nope. Ordered a hot tea and has been sitting there since. I'm not sure what is up."

"Thanks. Can you put two burgers in for us? Fries on both."

"Sure."

Daniel took his beer to her booth, and she looked up, shock filling her face. He slid into the booth across from her and smiled before taking a sip, not tasting the beer at all as he tried to judge her mindset.

"Are you following me?"

"I stop by here a couple of times a week. You left without saying goodbye."

"I left a note." Sophia looked like she was about to get up and run, but she deflated as Hank came over and placed ketchup, salt, and pepper on the table, along with two sets of utensils. Her brows wrinkled, and she started shaking her head. "Like this. You bought me food. I can't ever pay you back. I'll be in debt to you forever. I can't afford to eat at a restaurant like this. I barely—"

"You don't ever have to pay me back. I'm not doing this to get anything from you."

"Good, because I can't give you anything, and I won't…"

Sophia's voice died, and a shudder ripped through her. Something bad had happened to her, he would bet money on the fact. He wanted to help her, and he thought he was on the path of doing just that, and then she'd run from his work without telling him she was leaving.

"You can leave town later, but you can't sleep outside tonight," Daniel said.

Her lips turned down in a frown. "I have a tent."

"This storm could get bad, and your tent is thin. How low is it rated for?"

Sophia narrowed her eyes and shrugged. "What does that mean?"

Frustration ground through him. He needed Sophia to listen and listen well, but he didn't want to treat her like a child. He couldn't have her tromping out into the wilderness at this time of night. The sun was going down soon, and the storm would be raging by midnight. The temps were expected to drop thirty degrees in the next few hours. Even if she pitched her tent in the perfect spot, her being out there could lead to disaster.

Hank stopped by with their burgers, the scent reminding him he hadn't eaten enough today with all the physical labor he'd done. Sophia looked like she could devour the burger in just a few bites.

"Do you need anything else?" Hank asked.

"Thank you. I'm fine. Sophia, how about you?" Daniel asked.

She shook her head. "No. Thank you."

Hank left the table, and Daniel watched as Sophia stared at the burger. He thought she wasn't going to eat, but then she picked up a French fry and took a bite. She grabbed the ketchup, poured a dollop onto her plate, and began dipping the fries into the sauce, chewing slowly.

Daniel took a bite of his burger, moaning as the

taste filled his mouth. "Come back to the office and stay there. Once the weather is better, you can go wherever you want. I would feel responsible if something happened."

"I'm not your responsibility."

He set his burger down and shook his head. "No, you aren't, but I want to help you."

"Why?"

Daniel blew out a breath and took another sip of his beer, trying to find the words so they didn't sound wrong. Finally, he just shrugged and met her gaze. "Because I have empathy. I've seen people in bad situations, and I can't turn my back when I have resources and can help you. I'm not giving you anything for free. Not like I think you're a charity case and need a savior. You spent the day working for me. That deserves either payment in money or in reciprocating value. If you wanted a job, I'd hire you."

She shook her head, and fear flashed over her face. "Cash only."

Daniel paused, not wanting to confront her about her demand for cash-only employment. He wanted to ask her who she was running from. But what if he was wrong? What if she wasn't running from anyone at all?

He'd eaten about half of his burger when he set it down, his thoughts rebelling at her suggestion, knowing he shouldn't make her this offer. "If you clean my office and pick up around the shop, I'll pay you in cash."

She shook her head. "No, you're just doing that out of charity."

He wanted to tell her she was being ridiculous. She needed help, and she wasn't willing to take it. What did she want? "I'm not—maybe I am, but you need help. You have no place to go, and no roof over your head. Quite frankly, you don't seem like you should be homeless."

She took a bite from her burger and then narrowed her gaze. "What exactly should a homeless person look like?"

He kept his mouth closed, not wanting to get into a trap. "I can help you. Just let me do it."

Sophia was being unreasonable, and he wanted to demand she listen. But pounding away on the table, frightening her into obeying his commands, wasn't the type of guy he ever wanted to be. He couldn't talk down to her like she was stupid. No, he had to approach her like an equal.

He'd seen enough bad behavior from people in

the military, and he didn't want to ever be that type of guy.

But this woman was pushing him to a place that was beyond reason. He didn't know if she was too scared to listen or was heading out into the storm in some reckless urge to punish herself.

Daniel couldn't stand the idea of her being alone, freezing, maybe injured or hurt, and he had no excuse for his feelings other than he liked her and was possibly attracted to her. Which he knew was wrong. He should help her, not just because he thought she was hot, but because it was the right thing to do.

Being with Sophia all day had twisted him up, and he didn't know how to get out of this without making an even bigger mess than he already had. He needed to focus on helping her, nothing else.

CHAPTER SEVEN

Sophia knew she was arguing with Daniel just to argue. He was right. She shouldn't sleep outside tonight, but she had started to feel things for him, which made her very uncomfortable.

She couldn't trust Daniel because he was a man. She knew women could be deceptive and evil, too, but she'd learned the hard way that most men in her life just wanted to control her, and she was done being controlled.

The burger he'd bought her was way better than anything she'd found in a trashcan in her trek across America. There had been a good burger outside a restaurant in Knoxville, but this was better. She ate every last bite, even the French fries, though she was stuffed. She wasn't sure when her next meal would be.

"I get that you are trying to help, but I just can't." She wiped her hand on the napkin and placed it on the table. "I will be okay."

A guy stood up from the booth next to theirs. Shock filled her. She hadn't seen him take a seat and didn't know anyone was sitting that close. Serves her right for ignoring everything around her before Daniel came in. She'd been feeling sorry for herself, wondering when she would ever find a place to call home.

"Excuse me," the guy said.

"Hey, Drew," Daniel said.

"Hello, Daniel. I was listening to your conversation. Sorry, couldn't help it. You shouldn't be out in this. I know you don't know me, and you probably don't like people telling you what to do. Maybe you've had someone making unreasonable demands. I can tell you from what I know about this area after working as an officer for the Virginia State Police. Being out in this weather will only end one way unless you are very prepared. I'm sure you can manage on your own, but please, just take him up on his offer of hospitality."

Sophia's face heated, and she wanted to hide.

These guys weren't Brandon, and they weren't her brother.

Drew tipped his head and then tapped the table. "Dying in the storm won't be getting revenge on whoever you're running from. But—"

"I'm not running from anyone," spilled from her lips before she could stop the words. She could tell from their expressions they didn't believe her. Heck, she wouldn't believe herself. It was obvious she was running and making bad decisions based on the history she had with the men in her past.

"I only want to help," Daniel said.

Pain lanced through her, and she closed her eyes, trying to keep the tears from coming. She didn't want to die, but what did life have to offer her? Everything had been hard for so long, and here she was eating a burger with a total stranger who was working hard to make her life easier. He'd said she could live in his office for however long she needed. She had food, a shower, clothes, and a place to clean those clothes. This was better than anything she'd ever had before. It wasn't this good even when she'd lived at home before Brandon and his shit.

"I'm headed out," Drew said. "Be careful. This storm is going to be bad. There have been a few tornados in Tennessee and Kentucky. It's going to be bad here."

Drew walked away, and she was left with Daniel watching her. He wasn't frowning or smiling. His expression looked blank, like he wouldn't give up what he was thinking. "I'm not as pathetic as you think I am."

"I don't think you're pathetic at all."

"Then why are you helping me?"

He grunted, and she flinched—just like she used to cringe around Brandon. But this guy wasn't like him, and she'd just put him in a box like she was accusing him of putting her in a box.

"I'm sorry. I suck. I shouldn't judge you so harshly. You're right. You haven't tried to manipulate me into doing something I don't want to."

He placed his hands on the table, palms down. It was a posture of safety. He wasn't going to reach out and slap or hit her. He didn't have his hands balled into fists. He wouldn't reach across the table and pull her hair or slam her face against the table. His calm filled the air, making her realize just how reactive she'd become.

"We've eaten, and it's going to get bad out there. I'll take you to the office, and I'd appreciate it if you'd still be there in the morning. I'm not trying to tell you what to do, but I have a few jobs lined up for you over the next week. It's with people who need help. Some of it won't be easy work, but I think you're capable. As I said, you can stay at the office as long as you like. I don't expect anything from you."

She nodded, trying not to look away. The urge to hide filled her. She had no reason to hide from him. He hadn't done anything to her, just tried to help.

"I'm not going to lie and say I don't find you attractive, but Sophia, I don't want to push you into anything you don't want to do other than stuff that is for your safety. Once the storm is gone, if you want to leave, at least wait until after you've been paid for the cleaning jobs. You need money to survive in our world, and I'd like to know that you're surviving."

He stood up, and so did she, deciding to stay in Fallport for the time being. He held out his hand. At first, she wanted to shake her head no, but she took it as she slid from the booth. The warmth of his skin burned through her. It felt good, too good. It had been so long since someone had touched her with care. The last person who had touched her had been Brandon, and then he'd beat her so badly she thought he'd broken her ribs. That was the day before she'd run.

Tears threatened, but she held them back. The last thing she wanted to do was to make him feel even more sorry for her. The storm was the only reason she needed his help. She had survived on her own so far, and she would again once the storm ended.

She was grateful for the place to stay and the cleaning jobs he'd lined up. The money would come in handy. But that didn't mean she would stay too long after the weather cleared.

Daniel let go of her hand, and she drew in a deep breath, trying to hide her disappointment. She didn't need feelings. That's what had gotten her into this mess in the first place. She couldn't trust her gut because her gut had told her Brandon would be good for her. That had turned out to be a total lie. She was on her own, and she was fine with that. Now she just had to convince her libido she wanted nothing to do with Daniel.

CHAPTER EIGHT

Daniel woke to a winter wonderland. The nursery would remain closed today, and he texted as much to his employees. Once the sun rose, he would drive his truck over to his office as long as he didn't see reports of wrecks. The last thing he wanted was to cause more problems for first responders.

His phone rang, and for a moment, he wondered if it was Sophia, but no such luck. The caller was Zeke.

"Hey, man, everything good?"

Zeke made a noise that sounded like a groan. "No. Someone went hiking yesterday, ignoring the weather reports and all the warnings. We're headed out to find the person, but I wanted to let you know where we were in case you need to come out with another group to rescue us."

"Sure, send me your coordinates now and then whenever you get any signal. I'll be waiting to hear back from you. And Zeke, you guys stay safe."

"Sure. You know I normally wouldn't need—"

"Hey, no apologizing. The weather is bad, and another storm is moving in. If you need anything, text me. You know my truck can make it on the ice, and I have friends with snowmobiles. I'll do whatever I can to help."

"Thanks. I'll be back in touch with you later."

He ended the call, worried about Zeke and the rest of the gang. They were the best guys he'd ever known. He would be honored to become a member of their team, but it was nice to know they considered him a viable backup when life got hectic.

After the call from Zeke, he checked the weather and any alerts that were coming up. After the next wave of storms that should hit close to noon, they'd be clear until next week.

He cleaned his house, running the vacuum in rooms he usually forgot about cleaning. His stomach twisted with thoughts of the rescue happening right now and thoughts of Sophia. She could have been stuck out there with no one to help. The storm had been worse than they'd been predicting, and he had a bad feeling about the people the guys were going out to rescue.

After cleaning, he showered, trying not to think of the beautiful woman staying at his office. It was no use, and he took care of his hard-on before he turned off the water. He didn't want to be a disgusting jerk toward her. She needed a friend, not someone lusting after her.

Before the next wave of storms rolled through, he decided to head to the nursery. The town was mostly dead. Everyone knew to stay home and wait out the weather on days like today. He didn't blame them. He was only heading to work because Sophia was there, and he wanted to see that she was okay.

He'd grabbed extra gloves and a scarf before leaving home. He'd also brought his box of hot cocoa and marshmallows, hoping Sophia wanted some. Maybe he was making too much out of her sticking around, but he wanted to spend time with her.

He found Sophia cleaning the steps leading up to the office. She turned to watch him park his truck, then returned to get the ice off the steps.

"Thank you," Daniel said as he exited his truck.

She stopped shoveling and turned to face him. "It needed to be done."

"I brought some hot cocoa. Would you like to take a break?"

Laughter bubbled up, and he thought it sounded better than anything he'd ever heard. He wanted to make her laugh again but couldn't think of anything witty to say.

"I haven't had hot cocoa in ages. Maybe six or ten years."

"Well, you need some. Come on. I'll help you with the rest of the work once you warm up."

She narrowed her gaze but didn't argue with him. They stepped inside, and she removed the boots she wore. Her nose was pink, and when she took off her gloves, he saw that her hands were red from the cold.

He could talk her into watching a movie, maybe. He needed to be smart about how he went about this. From his previous interactions with her, he figured she didn't like being told what to do.

"I'll plug in the electric kettle and get it going," Daniel said.

"You don't heat your water in the microwave?" Sophia asked.

Now it was his turn to chuckle. "No way. I know people who get way too argumentative when it comes to heating water in the microwave.

Customers looking for the kettle find it, and people who don't care don't even notice it."

Sophia shrugged. "What's the difference? The water gets hot."

He made a shocked face and slapped his hands over his mouth. "My customers from Europe would be shocked."

"Are there many people living here from Europe?"

"A few. This area doesn't draw too many people from other countries, but it's not totally void of charm."

He turned and caught Sophia watching him. Her gaze warmed him like hot butter on popcorn. He wanted to reach out and pull her into a hug. He didn't. Instead, he just flashed her a smile, wishing they would be more to each other one day. Maybe all they would be was friends, but he would be fine with that, mostly.

CHAPTER NINE

Daniel smiled, sending warmth through her. She'd given up so much in the past. Hope seemed too far away, along with love and all the other good things most people cherished. This was her life, but maybe it didn't have to be. Maybe one day she would have good things again.

A trickle of excitement slid through her veins, making her want to reach out and touch him, but her history made that impossible. She settled for letting her hand flutter only a few inches away from her body, more like a twitch.

"I'm sorry," she said. "I shouldn't have run off like that. I was just..."

Daniel's eyes narrowed just a slight bit. Uncertainty slid through her, and she shrank from him.

"You were what?" he asked, his voice calm and low.

She closed her eyes, unsure if she wanted to get into how bad her life had been. "You just caught me off guard. I've not had many people be kind to me."

He nodded, understanding in his eyes. "It's okay. I'm just glad you're okay. The storm got wicked last night. We have another wave coming, but it's not going to be as cold. It should melt some of the ice. Everything around here will be a mess for a while, but we'll deal with it."

"So, the drive over, how was that?"

He poured the hot cocoa package into the mugs and held up the box of marshmallows. "One or two?"

"Two."

"Traffic wasn't bad. But then again, few people are out on the streets."

"I haven't seen anyone go past." She watched, curious that he was fixing her a drink. In all the time she'd been with Brandon he'd never done anything domestic.

"That's good to know. I'm glad people are taking safety precautions."

Daniel poured the water into the mugs and stirred before moving her mug where she could grab it. She took a sip and moaned.

"This is great."

"Yeah, I like this brand."

She moved to the kitchen table, but Daniel held up a hand, so she stopped. "Yes?"

"Do you want to watch a movie?"

She shook her head. "We still have ice to clear."

He nodded. "We do, but I think it's snowing again. We should wait for this round to end before we go back out there."

She didn't want to say no, but she felt awkward hanging out with him. He was a nice guy. He couldn't help it if she'd had a dream about him last night. She'd woken up wanting to do more than just kiss him, and that's when the heat of embarrassment hit hard. Feeling this way about him was wrong.

"There's a pizza in the freezer we can heat later," Daniel said.

This man intrigued her though he set her on edge. But why did he make her feel strange? He wasn't like Brandon, and she was sure he wouldn't hit her or do anything she didn't want. He was respectful and though she was alone with him, she didn't feel in danger. The edge she'd clung to every time she'd been alone with a man felt much duller with this guy. "Sure. That sounds great." The words came from her mouth like she'd meant to say them, but she'd spent her existence since becoming an adult never being alone with a male who wasn't her brother or Brandon.

If she'd sat on her couch and watched a movie while sipping hot cocoa with a guy and Brandon found out, she feared even thinking about what type of punishment she would have suffered.

Daniel turned on the TV in the room where she'd been sleeping—thank goodness she made up the fold-away bed. It would be awkward having him come in and see where she'd been sleeping and dreaming about him kissing her body. The thought heated her, and she had to push it away. It was wrong to think that way about this man, but the thoughts hit her again and again.

She worried he would pick a sexy movie, but he picked an action flick she hadn't seen. The movie kept her entertained for a good hour or so, but then hunger hit, and her stomach kept letting them both know.

Daniel paused the movie and stood. "How about that pizza?"

"Sure." Sophia stood, thinking he would want her to fix it, but he moved faster than she could and already had the stuff out to heat the pizza.

"I have some broccoli in here, too. Want some heated up?"

She shrugged. "I should. Broccoli isn't my favorite, but I can eat it."

"What's your favorite?"

"Brussel sprouts and asparagus. Broccoli is fine, but it's a little much for me."

"I'll cut back on how much I planned to fix."

"Oh, you don't have to do that. I just—"

Daniel set the pizza and broccoli on the counter and turned to face her. She thought he was going to take her hands for a moment, but he just held her gaze.

"It's okay for you not to like something and voice your opinion. You don't have to like what I do."

Tears threatened, and she turned away from him, not wanting him to see how much his words affected her. She'd lived for so long being told what to eat, how to eat, what she could drink, all of it, that having Daniel show her this kindness felt so out of place she couldn't believe he didn't want to control her. Living in a world without someone telling her what to do was a dream come true. She'd thought she would have to be alone to have autonomy, but here she was, crying over broccoli.

"Hey, it's okay." Daniel had moved closer, and his

hand was on her back, his touch light but producing so much heat she felt the flames licking at her stomach.

She glanced up, and their gazes connected. It was like someone had poured lava between them. The gasp that escaped her lips was followed by sparks in his eyes. She was sure he would kiss her based on how he leaned in, how his eyelids closed just a little, and how his hand got a little more possessive on her back. But his phone rang, interrupting them.

Daniel stepped away so fast she thought there would be skid marks on the floor. Of course, there weren't. To stave off the disappointment, she put the pizza into the oven and set the timer for nine minutes. That's when she started tuning into what Daniel was saying.

"Are the rest of the guys okay?"

Sophia turned, seeing the way Daniel's shoulders had deflated. He nodded and made a noise, then he shook his head.

"That's a damn shame. I'll be around if you guys need anything…okay, I'll talk to you later." Daniel ended the call and shoved his phone into his pocket.

She watched him, wanting to ask what the call was about, but a part of her didn't want to know. This man had a network of people he cared about and who cared about him. Back home, she'd been alone. Not one person had cared that she hadn't been seen in public for months, or that she had bruises on her face, or when she had broken bones or cuts and bruises. No one cared. No one came after her. No one wanted to help.

But Daniel had people stopping him at bars, giving advice on how to stay safe, calling him to make sure he was okay, updating him on things happening in their own life. It was odd.

"That was Zeke, the guy who owns On The Rocks. They had to do a rescue this morning. Someone went out hiking yesterday afternoon and didn't return. They went out on the Eagle Rock trail, and it was too cold."

"Wait, they didn't return, as in they died?"

Daniel met her gaze. A mixture of anger and caring shone back at her. "It was too cold, and they froze to death. The mixture of freezing rain, sleet, and snow was too much. They were soaked all the way through."

"Shit." Sophia slapped her hands over her mouth. She'd almost been like that person. She didn't know why she thought she could last through the storm. She'd been upset that it seemed like Daniel wanted something from her she wasn't willing to give, but here she was today, wondering if he would kiss her. She wasn't making sense, and her impulsiveness almost killed her.

Daniel's phone pinged with a text, and he checked it and then shook his head. "Sorry, I need to go help Cora Nichols. A tree limb broke, and they're afraid it will crush the porch and bring down that side of the house."

"You can't work in this weather."

He shrugged. "Probably not, but I'm going to check and make sure everything is okay."

Sophia reached back and flipped off the oven. "Hold on, let me put on my boots."

"You don't—"

"I'm coming with you. I may not look like much, and I may not be able to physically help, but I can help by looking out for you. Come on, we need to get there before the storm worsens."

Daniel's smile lit up his face. "Yes, ma'am. Let's go."

They locked up and raced to his truck, careful of the ice accumulated on the ground. She couldn't believe she was going out in this to help someone she didn't know, but that's what real community was about, right? Daniel had offered to help, and that was how she wanted to be. She hated her previous life and how she couldn't do much other than make sure Brandon wasn't unhappy, which was an impossible task. Here, she could do something that counted. Her heart squeezed. Why couldn't she have met a man like Daniel when she'd been younger? Maybe her life was looking up.

CHAPTER TEN

The branch was touching Mrs. Nichols' house, but from what Sophia could see, it wasn't bad. Only the thinnest part of the branch and smaller branches were against her house.

Daniel had gotten close to check out the roof, but because of the ice on the ground and on the tree, it didn't seem like there was much he could do until the weather cleared. She and Mrs. Nichols were standing at the back of the house, close to the garage. The falling snow had picked up, creating an almost whiteout condition. Sophia had flakes clinging to her hair. They needed to get inside, and Mrs. Nichols needed something to warm her up. She was about to suggest they wait inside when Daniel waved.

"I'm sorry, Mrs. Nichols, I can't get to it until the ice clears," Daniel called out. He was moving away from the tree but hadn't cleared the area when a loud snap sounded. Daniel took off running. His boots had some traction, but not enough. She saw him go down on one knee as a larger branch began falling, knocking smaller branches to the ground as it fell.

Panic filled Sophia, and she wanted to go to Daniel, but Mrs. Nichols grabbed her arm, holding her in place. She watched in horror as the limb slowly fell, taking out other limbs on its way to the ground.

The crashing and groaning sound contrasted with the snowfall's gentle hush. She had no idea if Daniel had covered enough ground not to be taken out by the branch crashing to the ground.

As an afterthought, she guided Mrs. Nichols into the garage, making sure she was safe before disentangling herself from the older woman and stepping out just in time to see that Daniel had made it to safety.

She moved to him, touching his arms and shoulders, then his face, to make sure he really was okay. His slow smile made her heart squeeze and her knees go weak.

"You're okay," Sophia said.

"I'm okay." Daniel turned back to look at the huge branch in Cora's huge side yard. "Shit, I thought I was a goner."

"You can't do anything until this storm is over."

Daniel nodded. "It's too dangerous. She should have taken this tree down last year, but she hated the thought of taking an axe to it. Now, this."

"Was it dead?"

"Yep. Now it will have to come down, but not today and probably not tomorrow."

Mrs. Nichols stepped out of the garage, her gaze narrowed. "What am I going to do with this?"

"Can you stay at someone else's house today? At least until the ice melts off the branches? It's going to be dangerous for a while. More of those branches will fall."

As if to emphasize his point, the crack of another branch split the air. She and Daniel flinched, and he pulled her close as they moved away from the tree. This one fell on the other side of the tree, filling the front yard with the downed branch.

After the branch had settled, and the only sound was the gentle falling of snow, Daniel met her gaze, and they both burst out laughing. He had his arm around her, and it just felt like the most natural thing to be in his arms.

Someone stepped out of a house across the street. "Hey, you two okay?"

Daniel waved. "We're good."

They headed into the garage and found Mrs. Nichols. Her lips were down in a frown as she shook her head.

"Do you have someone you can stay with until the ice melts off the branches of that tree?"

Mrs. Nichols shook her head. "Of course, there's Clara, but I don't want to impose."

"Why don't you call? I'm sure they wouldn't see it as an imposition," Daniel said.

She nodded as she made her way into her house. They stood in the garage, huddled close, his arm thrown casually around her shoulder. Excitement bubbled up. Was this how normal relationships worked?

Not that she had a relationship with Daniel, but he was being nice, not trying to come up with insults that would tear her down.

Just thinking of Brandon sobered her, and she stepped away and moved to look out into the yard. She didn't know if she would ever feel normal or what normal really felt like.

"The snow is really coming down now."

"I hope Mrs. Nichols can find a place to stay."

"She will. Someone will open their house to her."

The door opened behind them, and they both turned. The older woman had a frown on her face, and sadness filled her eyes.

"Well, it's done. I'm staying with Clara. They're on their way over. You two can take off. I guess that tree has to come down. I hate that. It has been here since I was born. It doesn't deserve to be taken down."

Another crack sounded as ice and snow brought down another branch. They turned to watch it fall. The tree was going to come down. Hopefully, Mrs. Nichols' house would be spared.

A car pulled up out front, and two people got out. They waved and then realized they couldn't get to the front door. After a few seconds, they got back into the car and drove around to the side of the house.

"That's my ride. Thank you, Daniel. And it was nice meeting you, Sophia."

"It was nice meeting you, too."

Daniel helped her out to the truck, and they took off, heading back to the nursery. She had never had anyone close enough to depend on. Anyone who helped her in her previous life had done so with strings attached. And some of the people who said they were helping were actually doing whatever the thing was for their own benefit. She'd never had anyone just help her.

Daniel parked the truck, and they sat in the front seat, watching the area turn even more white. "Looks like it's heavier now. I thought it was supposed to clear up," Daniel said.

"It's pretty."

He nodded and popped open his door. A cold blast of air hit, and Sophia opened her side and then tugged her coat tighter as she made her way up to the office door.

Daniel keyed open the lock, and they made their way inside, stopping to remove their boots, gloves, scarves, and coats. The room wasn't as warm as Mrs. Nichols' place, but it was much better than the truck.

"I'll turn on the oven and get that pizza heated."

"Sure," Sophia said. Her mind had drifted so everything seemed far away, distant in a weird way. This world Daniel lived in seemed unreal. People were nice to each other. They helped in so many ways. She'd never known that type of community. Where she came from, people were selfish. They took instead of giving. No one like Daniel existed back there.

The oven popped and clicked as it heated, and she took a moment in the bathroom. After she finished washing her hands, she stared at herself in the mirror, something she hadn't really done in a while. There were no bruises, no healing cuts, and the fear wasn't present in her eyes. Did she dare have hope?

"Hey, Sophia, do you want a beer or cola?"

"I'll take water."

"Sure," Daniel answered, and then she heard him walking away.

She closed her eyes, trying to hold on to this feeling. What was it? Hope? Did she dare have hope for a future?

The sun would set soon, and the roads would worsen as the slush froze again. The hope of having clear roads diminished as the storm refused to let up.

He glanced over at Sophia, who'd fallen asleep about twenty minutes ago. She really was beautiful, but he felt she didn't know it. When he first met her, she'd had a gray cast about her skin. Now, her cheeks were rosy like she wasn't approaching death's door.

When the pizza had finished heating, he'd seen the gleam in her eyes. He'd insisted she eat more than one slice, though she'd argued he deserved more. There was something in her background she wasn't telling people about, and he wanted to know exactly what the was.

They'd spent the afternoon on the couch together, watching movies and waiting for the storm to pass. It hadn't. Now he wanted to stay here but knew he had to leave. There was only one place to sleep, and he wasn't going to push for them to sleep on the same fold-out bed together.

Warmth filled his heart as a small snore came from her. He wanted to pull her into his arms and hold her all night, but that wasn't how things worked. He couldn't force her to do what he wanted because she had needs and wants of her own.

He checked the weather again and saw that the snow should stop in the next hour. He should already be at home, not causing any problems for first responders, but he hadn't wanted to leave Sophia's side.

Today had been good. They'd grown closer, or he thought they had. Maybe it was an illusion, but he liked it.

Sophia's breathing changed, and she blinked open her eyes, then rubbed her face. "Oh gosh, did I fall asleep?"

"You were tired. I need to head home. Lock up after I leave."

"Oh." Sophia sat up, wiping her face again. "Has the sun set already?"

"It will soon. I'll be back tomorrow. We probably won't be open tomorrow with the ice on the roads. That cleaning job is supposed to be tomorrow, but we'll need to see how the roads are."

"I could walk there," Sophia said.

He shook his head. "My truck can handle the roads, but I'm not sure about everyone else who thinks their little cars can."

Sophia's laughter warmed him. He had it bad for her. Maybe he needed to find someone but finding someone in a city this small was impossible. He didn't know everyone, but he knew a large percentage of residents, and he knew they gossiped like fiends. Already, he was sure Cora had told everyone she knew that he and Sophia were a thing. But they weren't, not like he would like them to be.

He blew out a breath and stood, knowing he couldn't solve this today. "I'll be back in the morning. Have a good night."

Sophia stood, and the urge to pull her close and kiss her made his lips tingle and his fingers itch to hold her. She wasn't his, he reminded himself for the tenth time tonight.

"Have a good night," Sophia said, her voice still filled with sleep.

Daniel resisted the urge to pull her into a hug and stepped out into the freezing cold. He'd been comfortable inside, and the icy wind was like a slap in the face.

He drove straight home and headed inside. His place was fine. Nothing was damaged or out of place as far as he could tell. He had trees in the yard, but none were on the verge of breaking or falling. Their limbs looked a little weighed down, but they were okay.

After checking his email, he showered and settled on his couch with a blanket pulled over his legs, and checked for any news on the city. He scrolled through social media posts, looking at the photos other residents had taken. There were two photos of Mrs. Nichols' yard, and you could see him hugging Sophia in one of them.

A weird feeling slid through him. He liked having Sophia close, but they weren't at the relationship point. Heck, they weren't even at the trying to do a relationship point. They were closer to friends, but maybe she was really just an employee. But she didn't work for him. She was someone he wanted to help and maybe build a friendship with.

Relationships had always been disappointing to him. He'd had a girlfriend when he'd been in the Navy, but she'd wanted something different from life. Then he'd met someone he thought could be relationship material, but she'd refused to live in Fallport. It wasn't specifically Fallport. She didn't want to live in a small town, and he didn't want to live in Manhattan or Los Angeles.

Sophia was just someone passing through. He wouldn't get involved because being involved meant changing everything about himself, and he wasn't prepared to change.

CHAPTER TWELVE

The roads cleared up surprisingly fast. Without any clouds in the sky, the sun was able to heat the temperatures to a balmy forty-five by nine in the morning. At noon, after Sophia had enjoyed a warm breakfast, Daniel dropped her off at the house he'd arranged for her to clean.

She wasn't sure what she was expecting, but the woman met her on the porch, looking very apologetic. "I'm Honey, and I'm so sorry. I just can't handle this on my own."

Sophia went for a warm smile. "It's okay. I don't mind cleaning up messes."

"This is bad. It's my sister's house. She passed away a few months ago, and I didn't rush here to take care of getting it ready for market. I was busy, and there was really no excuse, but it had been a while since I'd seen her. Anyway—" the woman turned around and stared at the front door before turning back to Sophia. "I'm so sorry. I will pay you fifteen an hour, even if it takes the rest of the week."

Sophia hooked her arm in Honey's arm and turned her to face the door. "Let's take it head-on. That's the best way to deal with issues like this."

Honey walked through the door first, and Sophia followed. But they couldn't get past the entryway. Stacks of magazines and papers made it impossible to get through. What made it worse was two of the stacks had been knocked over, making it impossible to find any path.

"I guess she was a hoarder. She never wanted us to come over. Now I know why."

"You'll get some money from selling this house, right?"

Honey nodded. "Without looking inside, the realtor said we could get around two hundred thousand or more. That's a lot of money, but this house is huge. Sadly, I think it's going to take both of us more than a week to get it done." Honey slapped her hand over her mouth. "Oh gosh, I shouldn't have told you that amount. You're going to think badly of me."

Sophia shook her head. "It's okay."

"I loved my sister. She was a great sister. She always picked up the phone when I called. I just..." Honey trailed off and shook her head.

"It's really okay," Sophia reached out to comfort Honey.

"My husband lost his job. He was let go, and the insurance is killing us. I have diabetes and need my medication, but we can't afford the insurance. This will allow us to live. I don't have to stop taking my meds, and I won't die."

Sophia squeezed Honey's shoulder. "I know your sister would be happy knowing you'll be able to take the medication for your diabetes. That's probably why she left the house to you."

Honey nodded. "Most likely. She knew we were struggling after my Ed lost his job."

Sophia glanced around at the mess and shook her head. "This is a huge job. Do you have a dumpster ordered?"

Honey's eyebrows pinched together. "I didn't know I could order one."

"Let me call Daniel and see if he can help."

Sophia stepped outside and hugged herself tightly as a strong wind blew in. The grass in the shade still had ice and snow clinging to the blades, but the walkway and the streets were mostly clear.

She moved to stand in the sun, hoping it would warm her.

"Everything okay?" Daniel asked when he answered. He sounded anxious.

"Um, yeah. I was just wondering if anyone rents dumpsters."

"That bad?"

"It's her sister's house. If she wasn't getting good money for the house, I'd tell her to hire a bulldozer operator and junk it."

"Oh no. I'm sorry. I didn't—"

"Don't apologize. I don't mind hard work, and this is paying well."

"Okay, um, let me see what I can do."

"Sure."

She went back inside and decided they had to start somewhere, so they began loading boxes full of magazines. She was glad Honey had brought small boxes instead of huge ones because there was no way they'd be able to carry them anywhere.

Her phone rang, and panic flashed for a second until she saw Daniel's name on the screen. "Hello," she said as she answered, forcing a calm she didn't feel.

"Hey. I contacted the trash company. They want to know if it's trash or recycling."

"A large amount is recycling, but we can't even get past the front room so there could be a lot of trash."

"Okay. I'll call them back. They'll bring out a large bin for recycling and one for trash in the morning. Just make sure to tell Honey not to park in the driveway."

"I will. And thank you so much."

"Sure. Do you need me to come over?"

"Not right now, but we might need some furniture moved later. I'll call you if we do."

"Sophia, thank you."

"For what?"

"Sticking around."

She didn't know what to say after that. Why did Daniel want her to stick around?

He ended the call, and she shoved the phone into her back pocket, her mind still on him thanking her. They didn't know each other, and if he knew how big of a mess she was, would he be thanking her or telling her to leave immediately?

Her track record with guys was bad. She'd only had one guy, and he'd proven to be a total jerk. Maybe Daniel was a good guy, but did she even want to stick around and find out?

CHAPTER THIRTEEN

Daniel could see the exhaustion on Sophia's face. She'd worked hard for Honey, filling both the trash dumpster and the recycling one. They'd had to order a second trash dumpster. He'd found someone who restored baby furniture and was happy to take the furniture to upcycle it. Because it was so old, he paid top dollar, which he'd been there when Honey turned around and handed half the money to Sophia. At first, she'd said she couldn't take it, but Honey had insisted, saying that her sister would want Sophia to have it so she could be free.

Daniel had heard those words and not understood what she'd meant. Who was Sophia supposed to be free from? It wasn't him, surely. Then again, he didn't begrudge a woman her independence. If someone wanted to be free, he would support them. He would help Sophia however she needed help, and he expected nothing in return. If she walked away, it was her prerogative. However, if she showed any spark toward him, he would damn sure let her know how he felt.

He was set to pick her up at four in the afternoon. She'd spent five days helping Honey, breaking one afternoon to clean for the other family he'd arranged for her to help. The other family was a weekly job, and Honey understood Sophia needed to keep up with work that would be consistent.

He arrived out front of the house they'd been working on, smiling at the neighbors' decorations. There were pumpkins of all sizes and large spooky inflatables. It was directed more toward kids, but he bet a lot of teenagers would stop by this house. Candy was candy.

When he lifted his hand to knock, Sophia flung the door open. She had a champagne flute in her hand and a huge smile on her face.

"We did it!" Sophia declared.

Honey lifted her glass and flashed a smile. "The realtor came by an hour ago and approved everything. She said the place should sell soon."

"Good."

"Want to have a walk-through?" Sophia asked.

"Sure."

The windows were all open a little, even with the chill outside. Daniel understood why, though. Every room had been scrubbed clean and then painted. Sophia had said they were bringing in two guys to help, but he hadn't asked why. She'd gone from being totally dependent on him for all the answers to getting information on her own. He liked that she felt comfortable calling and hiring the people she needed to get the job done.

"This place looks amazing." Daniel turned to meet Sophia's gaze. "It looks great."

"Thank you. We helped paint a few of the rooms. I've never painted before, and the guys, it was a father and his son, taught us both so many tricks. I enjoyed the task, but I'm still sore."

He made a note of that for later. Not that he would rub her back, but maybe she needed an ice pack or something.

"The realtor was so happy we were able to make the place look so good and smell almost brand new."

"It does smell so much better." The first time he'd entered the house, he'd been shocked by the stench. Sophia assured him they'd opened the windows for fresh air as soon as they could make it to the wall.

They'd been lucky to only find a few dead rodents and nothing really scary.

He admired her for getting through cleaning a place like this, and he was glad her steady cleaning job he'd arranged wasn't this bad. This was more money, but there was no way it would be a steady income to clean out houses like this.

"This place looks really good," Daniel said as they finished the tour. The space was good, and the neighborhood was great. The yard was big enough for a garden, and he could have a tool bench in the extended garage.

It would also allow him to rent one of the rooms if he wanted. His gaze swung to Sophia. She had mentioned renting at one point, saying that soon she would need to find a place to live. They'd been interrupted by an employee coming into the office so he hadn't been able to answer her, but now, he wondered if he should look into buying a bigger place.

His current home was a rented apartment above a dry cleaner. He wasn't there during the day, so the dry cleaner operation didn't bother him, but he wanted a place to call home.

Later, he would call the realtor. Maybe they

could come to an agreement before the house went up on the market.

"Are you two ready to eat?" Daniel asked.

Honey's chuckle filled the room. "Oh, I can't. I need to get home. This took longer than I'd planned, and I need to return to my life."

"Thank you for hiring Sophia," Daniel said.

"Yes, thank you." Sophia pulled Honey into a hug.

They seemed to have created a bond while they'd been working together. He liked that Sophia had someone she felt close to. When he'd first seen her in the coffee shop, she'd looked so alone. He wanted her to put down some roots, if only for her own good.

When Sophia stepped back, Daniel saw moisture clinging to her eyelashes. He wanted to pull her close to comfort her, but he didn't want to embarrass her in front of Honey.

Once they were in his truck, he glanced over. "Would you like to go out for dinner?"

She shook her head. "No, I'm filthy. I'd like to shower."

"Okay, so how about you come to my place and—"

Sophia placed her hand on his arm. "All my stuff

is at the office. I need to change, too. I can shower there, then walk into town and meet you."

"There's no reason for you to walk into town. I have plenty of stuff to keep me busy at the office while you shower."

Sophia nodded, then glanced out the window, her cheeks pinking up. He smiled to himself, thinking that maybe she liked him. He didn't want to get his hopes up and blow this out of proportion, but at least now he felt he had a chance.

CHAPTER FOURTEEN

Sophia showered and dressed quickly. Daniel came back into the office seconds before she stepped from the bedroom. She and Honey had gone into town to grab sandwiches one day, and she'd seen a dress in the window on sale. The original price had been way outside her means, but she felt she could afford to buy the treat on sale.

Honey had said she looked great in it, so she'd bought the dress, wanting to save it for something special. This seemed like something special. Maybe Daniel didn't want anything with her, but she wasn't dressing nicely just for his attention. She wanted to look good for herself.

Daniel's gaze traveled over her, his smile spreading slowly. "You look great."

Her face heated, and she wanted to hide. Instead, she smiled. "Thank you." She wasn't good at accepting compliments, but that was because she'd received so few. A part of her didn't believe that Daniel thought she was attractive, but Honey had mentioned more than once that the way Daniel looked at her showed his interest.

Maybe Daniel was interested in her, but what good could come of them being together? She couldn't lose focus and allow herself to be swayed by something that wasn't real. Not that she'd ever had anything real in her life, but if she planned on staying here, she needed to make sure Daniel really did want her as more than just a maid.

"Are you ready?"

She nodded, shyness filling her. "Yes."

Daniel grabbed his jacket from the hook and then helped her into hers. They headed to town and to On the Rocks. "We don't have many places to eat in town."

"This is good. I like the food."

"It's a good place. I'm glad we have somewhere to eat. Halloween is coming up soon, and a lot of people decorated this year. I like the fun stuff some of the businesses put up."

"I noticed the neighbors decorating while I was cleaning Honey's house. I bet it's nice to live in a neighborhood like that."

"My apartment isn't set up to receive trick-or-treaters. I think the business will participate in the yearly festival, handing out some sort of treats. It's a fun holiday."

"It is. I didn't do much trick-or-treating when I was younger."

"Really? So no candy crash on November one?"

Sophia shook her head and laughed. "No. Not at all. My dad didn't like me having fun."

Daniel met her gaze and reached over, squeezing her hand. "That sucks."

He pushed open his door and hopped out. Daniel had made it halfway around the front of his truck before she even had her seatbelt off. He opened the door for her and helped her out. They headed into the restaurant and sat in the same booth they'd occupied before. This time she didn't feel the need to keep an eye on the door. The fear of being found had faded. Brandon didn't know where she was and couldn't find her.

They ordered food and drinks, beer for Daniel, and iced tea for her. Daniel took a long drink from the beer and then set it down. His gaze met hers, and the smile he shot her way made her stomach tighten.

"Have you thought about opening a bank account?"

The fear came back, and her muscles clenched. She shook her head. "No."

"Oh."

She hadn't told Daniel she was running from someone. In fact, she'd denied it on multiple occasions, and she didn't want to talk about it. But it was obvious that Daniel had guessed why she was here in Fallport and why she had no money.

"Hey," Daniel said as he reached across the table and lifted her chin. "It's okay. We'll figure out a way to keep your money safe."

She nodded, then glanced away. "I-I just don't…"

"You don't have to tell me anything you don't want to."

Her gaze swung back to his. "You're way too nice."

"I'm just average. People should be nice to each other. It's how the world keeps working. Selfishness shuts down progress. We'd all die out if everyone was selfish."

The plates of food came out, and they stopped

talking for a bit as they started eating. Sophia had chicken and mashed potatoes, and Daniel had a steak. The food was delicious, and she was about halfway through her meal when Daniel brought it up again.

"I think you need to do something to keep your money safe."

She bit her lower lip. She would have to tell him something so he understood. She'd emptied her account and closed it, but she knew she couldn't set up an account with that bank. They might make a mistake and send her something in the mail to her old address.

"You can think about it. You don't have to do anything now."

She nodded, but inside her head, worry had blossomed. How could she put down roots anywhere? What if Brandon found her? What if he came here and tried to take over her life? She would be screwed.

For the last few weeks, she'd been living so she could easily run, but Daniel had been so nice, and he'd helped her so much. Then she'd met Honey, who only lived about an hour or so away, and Zeke and a few other nice people in town.

That was the issue. She craved nice. She wanted to live in a town where people waved and said hello. She liked stepping into the coffee shop and having people say hello. It made her feel like she belonged because she'd never really belonged anywhere before. She needed this town, and that scared her.

CHAPTER FIFTEEN

Maybe it had been a mistake bringing up the bank, but he didn't like her having her money lying around. Someone would have to know she had money at the office, but what if someone figured it out? What if they decided to come after her and take everything? Cash wasn't recoverable when stolen.

When he'd dropped her off the night before, she'd seemed distracted. For a little while, he'd thought he could kiss her goodnight, but now she seemed too cut off. He wanted more information about her, but he wasn't going to dig.

The week had flown by, and Halloween would be the next day. Most of their decorative gourds had been sold, leaving them with the few that didn't look great. A customer came in and asked to buy most of the rest. He said he wanted to decorate with them for Halloween. Sophia boxed them up after the cashier had wrung them up.

She'd set her phone on the register stand and began boxing up the gourds. She turned away from the register to pack the boxes in the man's car. Her phone buzzed. He wasn't trying to look at her information. His eyes slid toward the buzz, and he spied a text with all capital letters. The person on the other side of the text demanded she come home, or he would hurt her. The man said some rather unkind words, stating that he would hunt her down and she would never escape.

He picked up the phone before anyone else saw the text and shoved it in his pocket. He helped her load the rest of the gourds into the back of the customer's car. When the customer drove off, instead of heading back to the shop, he grabbed Sophia's arm and guided her to the far side of the lot where there were no customers or employees.

"Everything okay?" Sophia asked, her brows bunched together.

He shook his head. "I don't think it is."

She reached out, her hand gently brushing my arm before she pulled her hand back. Her gaze slid away, and her lips pursed tight.

"Your phone was on the register stand."

"Oh," was all she got out.

"He texted you. Someone named Brandon."

A slow hiss escaped her lips, and she shook her head. "No."

"I want to help you, but I can't if you don't tell me what's going on."

Sophia turned and started walking away, then she spun back. "Why were you spying on me?"

With a heavy sigh, he shook his head. "I wasn't spying on you, Sophia." He took a step closer to her, trying to calm the quaking in his stomach at the mere thought of this Brandon person possibly hurting her. She was young and vulnerable. She didn't need to keep running. "I just happened to see your phone on the register and saw that text. I know you're scared, and I'm here to help you with whatever that situation is."

Sophia stared at him for a long moment, her brows furrowed as though she was sizing him up. She shook her head, and he saw the confusion swimming in her eyes. Finally, she let out a deep breath and nodded slowly. "Okay," she said softly.

"Whatever is going on, I want to help." He didn't want to scare her, so he kept his voice soft when he really wanted to roar and scream. "Who is this Brandon guy?"

Sophia bit her lower lip and closed her eyes. The pain that flashed across her face made him want to pull her close and never let her go. But he wasn't the type of guy to force a woman into anything. He prayed she would take his offered help.

Her hands twisted together, pulling at the skin, her fingers slapping together when she pulled them apart. The frustration was off the charts, and Daniel feared for her. When she met his gaze, the desperation was palpable. "I don't know what to do. He didn't start off hitting me. Then it got so bad I had to run. He has my number but doesn't know where I am. He keeps threatening me. At one point, I'd thought he was watching—that he'd figured out where I'd gone, but he hadn't. I'm afraid he'll hurt me even worse if he ever finds me."

Daniel frowned, his heart sinking at the thought of Sophia being trapped in a toxic relationship with no way out. He knew there were resources available that could help her get out of the situation, but Fallport might not have as many resources as a large community would. He would have to be the one to help her.

"Look, I know how hard it can be to break free

from an abusive partner," he said gently. "But you have to trust me. Okay?"

She didn't say no, but she didn't verbalize her yes. She only nodded.

"Good. I want to help you escape Brandon so you can start living without fear."

Sophia stared at him in surprise, clearly not expecting him to offer real help. Sophia needed someone on her side, someone who truly cared about her well-being and happiness and was ready to fight for both.

Daniel felt his resolve strengthen as he gazed into Sophia's beautiful brown eyes. He would do whatever it took to get her safely away from Brandon, even if it meant putting his own life in jeopardy as well. Sophia was worth it.

CHAPTER SIXTEEN

Sophia didn't know what Daniel could do besides everything he was already doing. He said he wanted to help but probably didn't know how big of a task that would be. If Brandon found her, he would kill her. She would forever be checking over her shoulder, no matter where she lived.

"Tell me about him," Daniel said.

She closed her eyes, not wanting to think about or talk about Brandon, but for Daniel to help her, she had to tell him all of the pathetic and gory details.

"I didn't know better—"

"Hey," Daniel cut her off and bent a little to look into her eyes. "Don't blame yourself for anything. He should have been truthful about his intentions."

His words were hard to take. Maybe she shouldn't have known better, but she'd bought into that mentality.

Tears filled Sophia's eyes. "He'd been charming in the beginning. I hadn't been ready for the first time he hit me."

She saw Daniel's fists clench, but he blew out a slow breath, calming slowly.

"I broke ribs, my arm, got concussions—"

"You mean he broke your arm and your ribs."

Sophia blew out a breath. "I'm not used to talking about it this way. He hit me. I couldn't do anything right. Eventually, I was a prisoner in our home. I had no friends, no life, just me doing everything for him."

Daniel nodded, his gaze expectant. "Tell me about all of it."

She'd hid this part of her life from everyone. It was weird talking about it. Maybe she should leave right now, but she'd grown used to having Daniel around, and she liked him. She didn't want to run from this place, too.

Her gaze rose and met his, holding it for a long moment before she began speaking quietly. "Eventually, every perceived slight or imagined transgression against him resulted in me being hit or punished."

Daniel's jaw tightened, and he nodded for her to continue. She wasn't sure she wanted to tell him more. He seemed so upset.

"At first, I'd been too afraid to speak up or leave, fearing that Brandon would come after me and kill me. Then the final beating happened, and I decided to leave. It took planning, but I've been afraid ever since."

"I won't let him get you ever again."

She blew out a breath and stared into his face. She didn't know him well, but she felt she could trust him with everything.

"I'm scared I'll make the same mistake again." She gasped and turned away. She'd said too much. Daniel didn't want to hear that from her.

He moved to stand in front of her and tilted up her chin. Looking into his kind eyes, she felt a surge of hope welling up inside her. At last, there was someone who cared enough to stand by her side as she fought back against the abusive jerk who had tried to take everything away from her. With Daniel's help, perhaps there was still a chance for freedom and happiness after all.

"I want more from life than just running from Brandon. I want someone special."

Daniel cupped her chin, and she thought he

might kiss her. He didn't. Instead, he pulled her into a hug and held on tightly. When he did kiss her, it was on the top of her head and not her lips. Some part of her wanted to tilt her head back and kiss him hard, but she had just gotten out of a bad relationship, though she hadn't loved him for a long time. The relationship hadn't really been a loving partnership. She'd been his servant at best.

Now with Daniel, she could have something special. But what if she screwed this relationship up, too? Did she dare hope that Daniel would want something with her? What if this was just him being nice? She really needed to figure out what kind of guy Daniel was, because there was no way she could deal with another possessive jerk.

CHAPTER SEVENTEEN

Daniel made sure Sophia was all tucked in, and the alarm was set before he took off that evening. He knew Brandon wasn't close, or felt like he wasn't because the guy had no clue where Sophia was. But that didn't mean he wouldn't figure it out.

As soon as Daniel hit the road, he pulled out his phone to call Anne, the realtor Honey had been working with. Once the woman answered, he mentioned the property, stating that he wanted to buy it.

"Oh, it's not even up yet on the market," Anne said.

"I'd like to make an offer," Daniel said.

"Okay. That's…are you in town?"

"Yes. I own the Shade Haven Nursery at the edge of town."

"Oh, that's right. You bought out the old nursery and brought in more exotic plants since you built those greenhouses. I remember hearing about it. That's quite an interesting business venture. So you want to make an offer on the house?"

"Yes, ma'am. I can stop by your office tomorrow—"

Anne's chuckle cut him off. "No time like the present."

"Awesome."

"My office is behind the bookstore."

"I'll be there in a few minutes."

Daniel drove to the realtor's office and stepped from his truck as Anne came out of the office door. She held up a folder and waved.

"I have the paperwork. Let's go to the house so you can look at a few things. There are some repairs you may not want to make."

"Sure, I'll see you there."

The neighborhood was lit up with Halloween decorations, but he didn't need the light to see the outside of the house. He knew what it looked like.

Anne exited her car and started up the walk to the front porch. "The biggest expenses will be the air conditioner and the water heater…I think. I've had an inspector in, and he thought the HVAC system would need some work. It's an older house, so that's expected. The water heater is in the garage and shot. If it had been in the house, I'd be worried about a leak. That has to be replaced before moving in."

"That doesn't sound too bad. I know an electrician and a plumber. I can find someone to help with the air conditioner."

"Okay, so that doesn't scare you. I want to show you the back deck."

"Sure."

Anne opened the patio door but blocked him from going out. "It's not super stable."

"I like working with my hands."

"This is an older house, but there aren't new neighborhoods springing up here like they are in the bigger cities. It will make a cute home for a family. Are you expecting to start a family?" Anne's eyebrows lifted then she waved her hand. "Don't mind me. I'm not like Cora, Ruth, and Clara. I won't go telling everyone and their dog that you are buying this house. It's a good neighborhood with lots of families and some older couples who've been together for years."

Excitement built in Daniel's chest as Anne took

him around the house, showing him the rooms he already knew because Sophia had given him a tour.

This house would be perfect. It had enough room for a vegetable garden in the back, and though the landscaping needed help, the yard was big enough that he could put in some plants. He'd already started a list of plants he wanted to bring over.

This would be a fresh start for Sophia. Now he just had to convince her to move in with him. Heat filled him, and he turned away from Anne, hoping he wasn't blushing.

"So, let's work up an offer."

Daniel gave her a generous number. He expected to go back and forth a few times. Anne shook his hand and flashed a huge smile.

"I'm sure Honey will be happy to hear someone has already made an offer. I'll talk to her tonight and get back to you in the morning. I have your number from your call. Is that a good phone to call you back on?"

"Yes, that's the correct number."

"Good, and good luck on the bidding."

He said goodbye, sitting in his truck, watching the area for a long moment after Anne left. Eventually, he started his truck and drove over to Zeke's bar. He'd been eating out quite a bit and should probably cut back, but his excitement was riding high, and he knew he wouldn't calm down for a long while. He needed to talk to a friend and make sure he hadn't made a mistake.

He thought about calling Sophia but didn't want to get her hopes up if the house fell through. Even if she didn't want to move in with him, he would still buy the house. He wanted to stay here. He wasn't going to move to another city because Fallport felt like home.

He stopped his truck outside the bar, glancing around at the large group of cars. He didn't recognize the vehicles and saw that more than half the license plates were from out of state, with about half of those being rentals.

The bar door opened, and he could hear yelling and screaming. Someone stumbled out, and another guy was pushed out before fists started flying. He rushed over, trying to help the waiter who sometimes said he was the bouncer but was obviously in way over his head.

Daniel came up behind the stranger throwing fists at the bouncer like he was a punching bag, and wrapped his arms around the man's chest, pinning his arms to the dude's side.

There was a lot of screaming and yelling. Daniel

feared he wouldn't be able to hold the guy still and prayed someone else would come to help him. It took about thirty, maybe forty seconds for Zeke to step out and assess the situation. The cops pulled up at about that time, and the guy he had a vice hold on stopped struggling.

"You can let me go. We aren't getting married," the jerk said.

"Don't hit anyone else. Just stand still and be a good boy," Daniel said as he slowly loosened his arms. He wasn't too surprised when the guy turned and tried to punch him in the face. But he'd been prepared and ducked so the dude punched the brick wall.

"Hey, Zeke, Daniel," the officer said as he moved in close and cuffed the man who'd just shown a brick wall what he was made of. Unfortunately for him, it hadn't been steel.

Daniel stepped away and was talking to Zeke when he heard the officer ask the jerk his name. The guy said something that sounded way too much like Brandon. Had Sophia's ex tracked her down?

CHAPTER EIGHTEEN

Daniel had to know more, but what right did he have to get the information from the cops? He would find out soon enough with everyone else when he looked at the police blotter in the morning.

Worry twisted his insides up so tight that when Zeke came over to shake his hand, he realized he was shaking. One of Zeke's eyebrows lifted as he narrowed his other eye.

"You okay, man?"

"Yeah." He nodded. "Yeah, I'm good."

"Come on in. Dinner is on the house."

"No, you—"

"Stop it. You saved my waiter. If you hadn't jumped in to help, he would probably be on the way to the hospital instead of getting patched up and sent home. I hate it when guys jump the workers. This all started because the dude wanted to chat with a woman who was there on a date with another woman. He wouldn't take no for an answer."

Daniel had no clue if that meant the guy was probably Brandon or not Brandon at all. "Did you catch the guy's name?"

Zeke shook his head. "I'll find out in the morning, or maybe sooner, if one of the officers comes in to talk."

Daniel didn't want to spill the beans that he was watching out for someone to come after Sophia, mainly because he didn't want the information ever entered on social media. God, he hoped no one posted about her on social media. He wasn't sure why anyone would, but people were weird.

"You look off today," Zeke said as Daniel took a seat at the bar.

He shrugged and shook his head. "It's all good."

"Is it that woman who looks like she's running from someone?" Daniel's eyes widened, and he was about to say something when Zeke held up his hand. "Don't worry, I won't say anything. Just because you're a good guy doesn't mean everyone is. There were tons of guys in the Army who were great, but then there were the turds who I couldn't trust. They took advantage of everyone whenever they could. Being stuck with one of them sucked. In military life, you can kind of make them pay for their stupidity, as long as you aren't too entrenched with them. Out here, you get in trouble for enacting revenge."

Daniel nodded. "I'd like to wipe him off the face of the earth, but I can't."

"Got it." Zeke took Daniel's order, then came back and sat on the stool next to him. "Once I get the guy's name who attacked my waiter, I'll send you a note. Later, once you get a feel of this woman, you can stop by and talk more so it's more than just you looking for this guy."

Daniel met Zeke's gaze and nodded. "That would be good. I'm worried that he will figure out where she is. I know he can't just track her down without hiring a private investigator. I don't know that he has the money to do that. But I fear he will find her just out of dumb luck."

"I get that. Trying to be rational when irrational things happen is hard."

A group of women came into the bar, and Zeke left to take their orders. His food came up, and he chowed down, wondering if he could search for information on Brandon without him seeing that someone was searching for him. He loved and hated technology. If he looked at some social media sites, it would track who had looked. He needed information, but he had to be careful how he got it.

Mistakes wouldn't be costly money-wise, but they would take a huge toll on Sophia. He wanted to protect her and keep her safe, so he had to be careful about his next move. The last thing he wanted was to be the reason why Brandon found her.

CHAPTER NINETEEN

Sophia had a hard time getting to sleep. She tried watching TV, then reading, but her mind kept tripping over thoughts of Brandon. He'd been so evil, so manipulative, and he'd taken advantage of her.

Was she making a mistake being attracted to Daniel? The man wasn't anything like Brandon, but in the beginning, she hadn't seen how evil Brandon had been. He'd drawn her in, then he'd changed.

Were all men like that?

Sophia flipped on the TV again and tried watching a show. When the show ended, she was going to turn it off, but the news came on and the first story featured a terrible storm in her hometown. The camera panned over neighborhoods that had been wiped out. The streets where she'd grown up, the area where her brother still lived, looked like they had been leveled.

Her stomach lurched. What if they were dead? Tears filled her eyes, and she brushed them away. Her brother was just as bad as Brandon, maybe worse. He knew Brandon had been beating her and hadn't cared. He could have forced Brandon to stop, but he hadn't.

She wanted to not care, to not wonder if her brother had been injured, but she couldn't just turn off all emotions like she would turn off the faucet. She wanted to be hard and jaded, but deep inside, concern still bubbled up.

That was the problem with caring. She couldn't turn it on and off like a light switch. If she could have been more jaded and angrier, maybe she could have saved herself some problems in the past.

She would have walked out on Brandon earlier if she could have turned off her emotions. He'd been a jerk, and she'd stayed because she cared.

Being strong enough to leave wasn't always the answer. Being detached enough to walk away also played a part. If she could have gone without looking back, she would have evaded so much pain, but she always looked back. Even now, she was looking back and wondering.

Was she doing the same with Daniel? Not that he'd hurt her, but was she giving him passes he didn't deserve?

She didn't think so. He wasn't a jerk. If anything, he'd been a gentleman from the first moment they'd met. He was helping her, taking care of her but not in a possessive way, more in a friendly manner. He'd helped her get jobs, helped her make money, and it seemed like he wanted her to have friends. Brandon had cut her off from everyone.

But there was still something nagging at her. Was she being naïve? Was he going to turn out to be a jerk, too, just like Brandon had?

The real question was, could she trust Daniel? Would he hurt her? She didn't think so.

She gnawed on her lip as she muted the TV and watched images from the storm flash on the screen. What she wanted to do with Daniel was crawl into his lap and be held. She wanted him to comfort her and tell her everything would work out.

Could they build something together, or would she end up getting hurt again? She wasn't sure, but there was only one way to find out—stay close and see what happened.

But deep inside, something prodded at her, telling her she should be careful. It was too soon to trust Daniel completely. She hadn't known him very long. Life wasn't always perfect, and he could hurt her just like any other man. She felt safe with him. But any man could turn. She'd felt safe with Brandon at first. Maybe this time, she would end up being happy.

Caution would be her game plan. She would keep all her walls firmly in place until she could be sure Daniel was a good guy.

She flipped off the TV and sighed. There was no way she could know that things would end differently this time, yet she had to hope. She wanted to believe that Daniel would keep her safe, not just in the physical sense of the word. She wanted him to look out for her heart, too.

She'd fought hard against opening up and letting him in, but maybe now was the time to tell him everything. She suspected Daniel would be strong enough to face whatever came their way. And maybe if everything aligned correctly, they could find happiness despite everything she'd learned to be true about relationships with her ex.

She would talk to Daniel in the morning and open up to him. If she explained why she was afraid to open the account and feared planting roots, he might understand and help her cover her tracks.

CHAPTER TWENTY

Helping at the nursery was wonderful. She enjoyed learning about the plants and taking care of them. It was nice to be trusted to do a task without having someone looking over her shoulder, waiting for her to fail.

She pushed away the thoughts of her past life and focused on checking the moisture level of the plants. She was almost done with the plants at the front of the lot when a car skidded into the lot, the driver threw the vehicle into park and hopped out.

Sophia jumped back, fear filling her. She thought of running, but the woman covered the distance in seconds, her lips down in a frown.

"Where is he?"

Sophia shook her head, unsure who this strange woman was talking about.

"Where the fuck is he?" the woman yelled as she turned around to face the office. "I know you're here!"

Sophia noticed the balled fists as the woman stalked toward the office. "Who are you looking for?"

The woman spun and snorted at Sophia like a dog or other animal would. "You're fucking joking. You know exactly who I'm here for. The bastard hasn't called me in weeks. He should rot in hell."

Sophia froze. Memories of Brandon yelling at her pushed through, leaving her gasping for air. She backed away, and the woman came closer, her face screwing up in a scowl.

"Are you fucking him? Is that why he didn't call me?" The stranger reached out and tugged on Sophia's hair, pulling just hard enough to hurt but not hard enough to do damage. "Is he spreading your legs and telling you lies? Are you fucking my husband?" The woman scoffed and leaned in close. "Just wait until he hits you like he hit me."

Sophia took another step back, her foot coming down wrong on a rock that rolled to the side, causing her to wobble. For a moment, Sophia feared she would fall. She gasped for air as panic rose. This was just like how she felt with Brandon. He would push her around until she fell or was forced into a position where she couldn't defend herself.

That second, Sophia made a decision to stand up for herself. No longer would she just take the hate being dished out at her. She stiffened her spine, ready to tell this woman to leave, when the woman swung hard, clipping Sophia under the chin with her fist.

Sophia first noticed the blood in her mouth, followed by a flash of pain. Then she started falling as her head filled with fluff. The ringing in her ears made it hard to hear anything.

Suddenly she was surrounded by the people who worked for Daniel. Frank looked shocked, Bella looked like she was going to cry, and Will held the woman back.

Everyone looked to her left, and Sophia turned her head, trying to follow the direction they were all looking. Her vision was blurry, and she had to blink a few times to see Daniel's truck. He would fix this.

Sophia tried to sit up, but her head swam. The woman had clocked her hard and maybe even knocked her out.

The words they were saying didn't make it past

the ringing in Sophia's ears, but she could see that Daniel was pissed off. By the time she could sit up, the police were there, followed by the fire truck staffed by a couple of volunteer firefighters. She'd learned that they had their EMT license, so they at least could administer first aid.

"Miss, can you hear me?"

The question felt like it had come from far away. She turned to the guy, hating the light he was trying to shine in her eyes. "What?"

"What's your name?" His eyebrows rose, and he looked at her like a teacher would look at a kindergartner hoping they would get the answer right.

"Um, A—" The word died on her tongue. She wasn't Angela or even Sophie any longer. She was Sophia. She cleared her throat, hoping she could do this right. "Sophia."

"Okay, Sophia, do you know where you are?"

She blinked and saw the plants and the office building. "At the nursery. The plant nursery."

"That's good. Can you tell me what town you're in?"

She closed her eyes, trying to clear the fog. The first word that came to mind was the town she'd grown up in. She shook her head, clearing a little more of the fog. "Fallport."

"Good. I think you just got your bell rung. You should drop by the medical clinic, though."

"Are you okay?" It was Daniel's voice.

Sophia flashed open her eyes and met Daniel's gaze. "Who was that?"

Daniel blinked, confusion filling his face for a moment. Then he glanced over his shoulder, and Sophia could see the police car with the woman inside. She was still screaming and kicking.

Daniel's face twisted into a grimace, and I saw the truth before he said the words. That woman had been here for him. Not Frank or Will, but Daniel. She'd said he was her husband. Was that right?

Daniel shook his head. "She is someone I used to know."

"She said—"

"Excuse me," the EMT said. "You need to stay calm. Your heart is starting to race."

Sure enough, Sophia could hear the fast beep from the portable monitor they'd attached. She closed her eyes as pain slid through her. Daniel had a wife, and he was a liar. He was just like all the other men out there. No, he hadn't hit her, but was that next?

She couldn't trust anyone. There wasn't a good person alive. Tears filled her eyes, and she fought not to cry. She didn't want Daniel to see how weak she was. Now she had no place to live. She would be forced to go back to the street. Would she ever find a place to call home?

CHAPTER TWENTY-ONE

Daniel couldn't believe Sherie had tracked him down. It wasn't like he'd tried to hide from her, but he hadn't left information about where he'd gone. She'd been a huge mistake he hadn't realized until it was too late.

It took another thirty minutes for everyone to clear out. Sophia had gone into the office once she'd gotten up, and the firemen had left. He needed to talk to her, to explain Sherie.

He stepped into the office, kicking off his boots because this conversation would take a while. His past wasn't perfect, but Sherie pointed out everything he'd done wrong. She had been at a low time when he'd been thinking of home and wanting to be a part of something other than just existing in the Navy.

"Sophia?" Daniel said, hoping she would come out and he didn't have to hunt her down in the bathroom.

Silence greeted him. Fear flashed, and he moved from the main room to the hall with the bathroom and laundry room. Both were empty.

"Sophia?" he said a little louder as he moved to the room with the pull-out couch. "Are you in here?" He knocked at the door, and it swung open. The room was empty. She'd cleared out her things. When had she taken off?

The police had distracted him, asking questions about Sherie and where she'd come from. He only knew her whereabouts up until he left California and moved here. She was one of the reasons he'd left the west coast. He'd hoped she would never have the initiative to search for him.

"Shit, Sophia, where did you go?"

He called her number, praying she would pick up. She didn't. Then he texted her, telling her that they needed to talk. She didn't reply.

Where had she gone? He pulled on his boots and headed out to his truck, desperate to find her. His first instinct was to drive down the road to the highway, but he wasn't sure if she would leave Fallport. She had cleaning jobs, and she had money.

Even if she stayed, would she have enough money to live here? Not without someone helping. He didn't want to lose Sophia because of this horrible misunderstanding.

He searched the town, going into Zeke's bar, then the coffee shop, and a few other places before driving the road to the freeway. She wasn't anywhere he'd gone. He texted her again, telling her that whatever Sherie had said had been a lie. He didn't want to explain in text, but he feared he would either have to leave her a voicemail or type everything out.

It was around midnight when he made it back to his apartment. He hadn't found her, and that worried him. She'd been knocked out and most likely had a concussion. She should've gone to the clinic, but he knew she hadn't. He was totally screwed.

Daniel pulled up a browser and started looking for news about her. He didn't even know what to look for, but his searching turned up nothing. He was about to give up when he decided to text Honey. She and Sophia had become friends. It was late, and he didn't expect a reply, but one came through in seconds.

Honey: Sophia is safe here. She's upset, but she's safe.

Daniel: Whatever Sherie told her wasn't the truth. I just want to talk to her.

Honey: She's sleeping. You could come by in the morning. But I have to say, I won't push her to go with you if she doesn't want to see you.

Daniel: Fair enough.

Honey: Come by at eight.

Daniel: I'll be there.

Honey texted her address, and he entered the information into his calendar with the address. He could get a few hours' sleep if he could actually calm down enough to sleep. Worry filled him. Sophia was an awesome woman, and he had feelings for her.

Sleep didn't come easy, and once in it, his mind twisted up with what happened and applied enough fiction to wake him up with his heart hammering. He slumped back on the bed, his stomach in knots from Sherie showing up and Sophia leaving.

Daniel showered quickly and dressed in nice jeans and a plaid button-down shirt. His hands shook as he fixed the last of the buttons, as his nerves pitched high. Sophia had found out the worst thing about him. He hoped she would forgive him.

The drive to Honey's house didn't take him as long as he thought it would, and he arrived early. He didn't want to sit outside the house and look like a stalker so he headed to the front door. With his hand raised to knock, he hesitated. This could all go south so fast. He didn't want to lose Sophia but feared he already had.

After a few more seconds, he knocked, and Sophia answered the door. Her eyes were red-rimmed, and it looked like she had been crying. Daniel's heart ached to see her in pain. This was the last thing he wanted for her.

"Sophia, I'm so sorry," he said, reaching out to touch her arm. She pulled away fast, and he dropped his hand back to his side. "Please, just let me explain."

"Explain what?" she asked, her voice calm but laced with anger and hurt. "Explain why you didn't tell me about your wife? Explain why you let me continue to fall for you when you knew this would come back to bite me—us in the ass?"

Daniel shook his head, "It's not like that, I promise."

"What is it like then?"

Honey appeared behind Sophia and flashed a smile. "You should come in. I have coffee and biscuits."

Daniel nodded, and Sophia stepped back reluctantly, her lips turning down further as he entered Honey's house. He followed Honey and Sophia down the long hall, painted a calming shade of blue to the kitchen, his stomach in knots. All the calming paint and warm decorations wouldn't help him feel better.

He had to start from the beginning, hoping that Sophia didn't think him too evil by the time he finished telling the story. If he'd met Sophia when he'd been younger, he probably would have screwed up everything with her.

Honey poured the coffee and grabbed a plate of biscuits, a few cut and lavished with eggs and cheese, then sat down beside Sophia. He wished he could speak to Sophia alone, but he respected Honey for not abandoning her friend.

If he wasn't so worried, he would pick up a

biscuit with eggs and cheese, but he didn't know if he could stomach it. His palms were sweaty, and he dragged them over his thighs, wishing he could get ahold of himself.

"Tell me," Sophia demanded.

"I was young and stupid. I'd been in the Navy for two years and was feeling lonely. I went out with the guys, and we met some women at a bar. Sherie decided to attach herself to me. I didn't think I had a care in the world and went back to her place, thinking nothing would go wrong. I should have gotten a ride back to base and ended my night. I didn't. I had no idea what type of person she was. I dated her off and on for the next year. You've got to remember, I was in the Navy so a good portion of that year had been spent at sea. She texted me a lot more than I texted back."

"So you fucked her and forgot about her?" The condemnation in Sophia's voice was easy to hear.

"I wasn't smart. I didn't know much about relationships or people or how to really be with a woman. I didn't make good choices. So I stayed with Sherie even though I thought there were some weird things about her. I didn't plan on having a long-term relationship with her, so I didn't think it mattered."

Sophia took a bite of her food, her gaze never

leaving him. He hated how the next part of the story would make him look—hated that Sherie had done what she had.

"Like I said, I was stupid. I didn't leave though I knew there were problems. She liked to act wild, and she sometimes got a little riled up. I just thought it was an act. Like she tried to be this fun person all the time, but it got to be exhausting. I didn't see her for who she was."

Sophia narrowed her eyes and her nose wrinkled like she didn't believe me. "Who was she?"

"I woke up one morning after a night of drinking with her, and I was in tremendous pain. I didn't know what had happened. She was above me, her eyes bright like she was on something. I tried to sit up, but the pain was too much. I touched my chest, which was where most of the pain was centered, and came back with blood."

Sophia gasped, and her eyes went wide. It was the first bit of concern she'd shown since he'd started his story.

"Like I said, I wasn't smart. I should have seen the warning signs. Sherie needed help, like psychological counseling help. She had cut my chest in a design that she said meant we were married."

"What the hell?" Honey asked.

He shook his head and held up a hand. "I take full responsibility for not seeing it early. She was wrong, but so was I for staying with her when I knew something was wrong."

"Wait!" Sophia's voice was raised, and then she slapped the table. "Are you saying this woman cut you, did some sort of ritualistic wedding, then declared you married?"

"Yeah. I never agreed to marry her. We never went before a priest or judge or any other kind of officiant. I was there, passed out from too much drinking, and she cut into me. I don't know why I didn't wake up from her cutting me, but I didn't."

"Hold on." Sophia pushed her chair back and stood. She paced away from the table and then back. "Are you telling me that woman isn't your wife?"

He stood and held his palms wide. "Only in her mind. I'm not legally wed to her. I'm not even common law wed to her. She made up this ceremony and the design she cut into my flesh and decided we were married."

Sophia put both hands on the side of her head and rubbed them in a circular motion. "I have a headache."

"I'm sorry you found out this way. Once we'd been together for a bit, I was going to tell you. I swear. But it just never seemed like the right time. This is next-level weird stuff, and I hate that I didn't realize she was so off her rocker before Sherie decided we were married."

Sophia shook her head. "I don't know what to think."

"I don't want you homeless again. I need to know you're safe and not in danger."

She stared at him for a long moment, then blew out a breath. "What are we supposed to do? Is now the right time for us to even try to…?"

Honey stood from the table. "I'm going to go outside and check my plants. You two need to talk."

He waited until the door was closed before he moved to Sophia. "I'm sorry you thought I had done that—had a wife and led you on. I like you, Sophia, and I want you to come back to Fallport."

She shook her head. "What about that woman?"

"Sherie is too delusional to understand reality versus the fiction that runs through her mind. I didn't know she'd found me. And I'm sorry you were affected."

Sophia reached out and grabbed his arm. "Will she get the help she needs?"

Daniel stepped closer to her and cupped her face in his hands. He knew Sophia was a good person. He just didn't realize how good she was. She cared about Sherie getting help though she'd been the one to hurt her. "You're a good person, Sophia. I know that things have been moving fast between us. I'd like to see where we go. But you have to know, Sherie could come back and attack again."

"I'll be prepared this time."

"She needs help, and I think the only way she's going to get any help eventually is if you press charges."

Sophia sucked in a breath. "But then my name would be documented. I can't have my name listed on a police report."

"She doesn't deserve to get away with assaulting you." Guilt filled Daniel. When Sherie had cut him, he hadn't turned her in for assault. He'd gone to the doctor and didn't tell them what had happened. They'd treated him for the wound but hadn't insisted he file charges. They might have thought it had been another sailor or military personnel, and the questions had stopped. If he'd pressed charges, maybe Sherie wouldn't have come here looking for him. He hated that Sophia had been hurt by his past. He just wanted to make sure nothing else could hurt her.

CHAPTER TWENTY-TWO

Daniel's story was so far from what Sophia had thought he would say that she didn't know how to take the information. Then there was the issue of Brandon or her brother finding her. She couldn't ever go back with Brandon, and if he found her, she wouldn't have a choice.

"Maybe we can get the police to keep your name out of the file," Daniel said.

She turned to face him, not believing that was even a possibility. "How likely is that?"

He shrugged. "I don't know. But I think if we ask, they might do it."

"I just can't have my name out there. I don't want Brandon or my brother hunting me down."

Daniel stepped close, his brown eyes full of caring. She wanted to reach up and cup his face, but fear kept her from moving. What if he was still lying? What if he hadn't told her the whole truth?

She'd learned the hard way that guys couldn't be trusted. If she ended up trusting this man and he hurt her, she would be a fool. The last thing she wanted was to be a fool about this.

"I don't know."

"Will you come back to Fallport with me?"

Honey stepped inside, hearing the end of his question. She met Sophia's gaze and nodded. "I don't think he's like the other guy."

Sophia looked at Daniel, not sure what to say. Part of her wanted to say yes and go with him back to Fallport. She liked the town and the people, and she really liked Daniel. It would be nice to have someone she could trust who wanted to help her. But the other part of her was scared. Scared that he would turn out to be like Brandon or her brother and hurt her.

"I don't know." She moved to the window and stared out at the brown grass. For so much of her life, she'd been alone in misery. Finding Daniel, then Honey had made all the difference in the world to her. She liked having people who supported her and helped her.

Daniel reached out and took her hand in his. "Please, Sophia. I promise I will do everything I can to protect you. You don't have to worry about Brandon or your brother anymore. I'll make sure they can't hurt you."

Sophia looked into his eyes and saw the sincerity there. He wasn't a jerk who wanted to take advantage of her. She felt in her heart that Daniel could be trusted. She turned to Honey, hoping her new friend would answer her truthfully.

"Do you think I'm making a mistake going back?"

Honey came over, placed her hand on Sophia's shoulder, and squeezed. "Life goes by fast, and you don't get a second go around. I'm older, and there are things I wish I'd jumped on when I'd had the chance." Honey glanced at Daniel, then nodded. "I think this man is one of the good ones. He has made some mistakes and paid for them, but he's not a liar and isn't trying to cheat you. I think you can trust him."

Sophia held Honey's gaze for a long moment, then nodded. "Okay." She turned to Daniel and nodded once. "I'll go back to Fallport with you. I'm still a little iffy about the cops."

Daniel's lips spread into a wide smile. He didn't kiss her lips, but he did move close and kiss the side of her head. She'd made the right decision, or at least she thought she had. Daniel wasn't anything like Brandon. This wouldn't end with her regretting her decision. Returning to Fallport was the best thing for her.

They pulled up at the police station, and Sophia reached for Daniel's hand once he put the car in park. "I'm scared," she whispered as she stared at the front of the building.

Daniel turned to face her and cupped her chin. "It is going to be all right," he promised. "I'll keep you safe."

She didn't say anything but wondered if anything could keep her safe. Brandon hated losing, and he'd lost her. She should have run from him years ago, but at least she'd finally left.

The officer on duty looked up when they stepped inside. "Can I help you?" he asked.

Sophia cleared her throat and met the officer's questioning gaze. She swallowed, fearing the whole process that was before her.

"I was the person assaulted at the nursery yesterday."

"Ah," the officer said, then spun to grab a folder.

"Yeah. I have some stuff for you to sign."

Sophia bit her lip as she looked down at the piece of paper with the name Sophia scrawled in the spaces referencing her. That wasn't her name. She didn't want to tell anyone her real name. It would open her up too much.

She couldn't file this report with a fake name. That would be illegal. "I-I…"

"What?" the officer asked.

She shook her head as she pointed at the piece of paper. "I can't sign this."

"What?" Daniel asked.

"Why can't you sign it?" the officer asked.

She hated revealing her name, revealing to Daniel that she'd lied about her name. She swallowed and closed her eyes. If she didn't file this report, then Sherie could return and hurt them again and again. She knew a police report wouldn't stop someone if they wanted to hurt her, but it would eventually make it more difficult for them. Eventually, they would be in jail long enough they might change their mind about hurting others.

She'd never filed a report when she'd been with Brandon. It didn't help that his friends were cops, but she should have done something. Maybe she would have been able to escape earlier if she'd been brave enough to file.

"Is there something wrong?" the officer asked.

"That's not my name."

The officer's lips turned down. "Filing a false report is a felony."

Right then, Sophia almost turned around and walked out. Daniel put his arm over her shoulder and held her in place.

"It's not a false report. No one got her name right, and they didn't ask. If I remember correctly, the officer never asked Sophia for her name. They asked everyone else but not her."

The officer's lips pursed tight. "What is the correct name? I'll have a new copy of the report printed."

Sophia glanced at Daniel and then swallowed over her fear. "Angela Sophie McDonald."

Now the officer knew, and Daniel knew. She prayed this didn't come back to bite her. She couldn't read the expression on Daniel's face, but he probably felt betrayed. She knew she would.

The officer told them he would be right back. She leaned her elbows on the high desk and closed her eyes. Daniel's hand on her back, massaging away her stress, made her eyes flash open. She turned to stare at him.

"Do you hate me?"

"No, I don't hate you."

"But I lied about my name."

He shook his head. "You were trying to protect yourself."

"I feel like I've made so many mistakes."

"Same. I feel like I should have told you first about Sherie."

"How could you have known she would come after you?"

Daniel shrugged. "I should have known she wasn't done with me."

The officer came over with a new printout. "Read this over and sign it."

"So, is there any way of keeping my name out of public documents?" Sophia asked.

The officer shrugged. "The report will be made public. That doesn't mean anyone will be looking at it."

"I just…" She trailed off, feeling defeated.

"Listen, I doubt anyone will come around looking for information. If they do, I'll black out your name."

Sophia nodded and then signed her name to the

report. She couldn't help but worry about having her name out there. But eventually, she would have to live again. Brandon had tried to dictate every part of her life when she'd been with him, and if she didn't file this report, it would be like he was still doing it.

CHAPTER TWENTY-THREE

They were back at the nursery, Sophia putting her clothes into the other room, when his phone rang. Daniel pulled the device from his pocket and answered.

"Daniel here."

"Hello, Daniel. It's Anne. I wanted to tell you the offer has been accepted."

His heart sped up. "Really?"

"Yes. They want to secure funding as quickly as possible."

"That's great. I contacted a bank, and I should hear back today."

"Good. Keep me informed."

He turned around and saw Sophia standing in the doorway. "What's the good news?" Sophia asked.

"I decided I wanted to live here more permanently so I put an offer on a house."

Her eyes widened and he wanted to go to her and pull her into a hug. He didn't move.

"You did? That's great!"

"Yeah, I should have said something to you, but then everything happened."

"Which house?"

"The one you and Honey cleaned up and painted."

Sophia's jaw dropped open. "You're kidding me."

He shook his head. "Nope, no kidding. I'm serious. I would like it if you moved in with me." His face heated by about a million degrees. "Not with me like that, but if you would live in one of the rooms. You would have your own space, and it wouldn't be at the office."

She nodded slowly. "So I'd be your roommate?"

He thought he saw disappointment filter over her features. "I don't want to pressure you into anything. I want you here because you want to be here."

She looked away, then nodded. He couldn't take her being disappointed, so he moved to her. His hands cupped her face, and he lowered, planning on giving a sweet kiss. But that's not how it went. Their lips pressed together, and their tongues tangled in a molten hot seduction that had him panting for air.

He pulled out of the kiss and stared down into her upturned face. She was the most beautiful woman he'd ever been with; it was more than just the outer beauty. Her soul was good, making everything else about her even better.

He leaned in, pressing a sweet kiss to her lips. He deepened the kiss, his hands tangling in her thick hair as their bodies pressed closer together. They fit together like two puzzle pieces.

She moaned and pushed against him, making his blood pound harder. Desire surged through him. He should walk away, but he didn't want to.

Daniel leaned back and met her heated gaze. She pumped her hips and brushed her body against his hardening length. He gasped, and she moved closer.

"Sophia, are you sure?"

She dropped her head back and exposed her long neck, and he could see down the V of her shirt, right to the lace of her bra.

"Yes, Daniel. I'm positive."

He lifted her, and she wrapped her legs around his waist. They were smiling at each other, and he wished they were already naked.

Daniel carried her into the other room where the

pull-out couch was. The bed wasn't out, but the couch would do. He lowered, and she moved quickly, falling to the cushions, a chuckle escaping her lips. He needed to feel her, touch her, and make sure she knew how he felt.

"Let's pull out the bed," Daniel said.

"If you wish, but I'd take you here."

He moved close, pressing his lips against hers in a fevered kiss. She grabbed his pants, undoing the belt before snapping open his jeans. Then her fingers were on his zipper, tugging it low.

He stood and pulled her up, tossing the couch cushions to the corner before pulling out the bed. She'd tugged her shirt overhead, and he watched in fascination as she popped off her bra.

His cock went full stiff as she reached up and squeezed her breasts, leaving the nipples exposed through her open fingers.

"Fuck, that's beautiful."

Sophia giggled again, and the sound shot straight to his cock. He moved around the end of the mattress and over to her, pulling her close so he could feel her whole body pressed against him.

"I need you," Sophia groaned when the kiss ended.

He didn't want to disappoint so he helped her out

of her clothes, then lowered her to sit on the edge of the bed as he pushed her feet about shoulder-width, then leaned in and licked up her slit. She had a small patch of hair, but not much, and he licked again, loving the taste of her. She moaned when he placed his mouth over her mound and sucked on her clit.

"Oh God," Sophia said as her fingers tightened in his hair.

Daniel chuckled, then sucked more. Making her writhe in his arms. She was so close to falling apart, but he wanted to extend her pleasure.

When he pushed her away, she groaned. "No, more," she begged.

"I'll give you more," Daniel said as he stood and shoved his pants low. He kicked off his shoes and then stripped off all his clothes.

Sophia's mouth fell open as she stared at him, taking in every inch of his body. He felt self-conscious for a moment, but she moved close and dropped to her knees.

Now it was her turn to torture him with her mouth. Her tongue did wicked things as she licked his balls and cock, making him harder than he'd ever been.

"Sophia," he ground out between clenched teeth.

She pulled off him and smiled. "Do you like?"

"Hell, yes. Maybe a little too much. Right now, I need to taste your skin again."

He pulled her to the mattress, lowered his mouth, and captured one of her rosy nipples. She gasped and arched up. Her soft hands slid up his back and over his shoulders, clutching at his skin before her fingers tangled in his hair, pulling him closer.

He moved to her other breast and sucked on her nipple, loving how she gasped and moaned as he made love to her. That's what this was. They weren't experimenting or fucking. They were making love.

He worried that his rough whiskers would be too abrasive on her soft skin, but she seemed to like it when his chin grazed over her. He trailed kisses along her jawline down to where her shoulders beaded with goosebumps. He licked over the spot, and she moaned and pressed her body closer to him.

He sought more skin and sucked and kissed until he reached that sweet spot below her earlobe. She gasped and arched up against him, one ankle hooking behind his leg.

She adjusted her position, and his cock brushed against her heated skin. With a growl, he moved fast and found her center, his lips and tongue licking and sucking until all she could do was make unintelligible sounds as she pumped her hips.

Her muscles clenched below him, and her words turned to begging as she pressed up harder. A low groan rolled out his mouth, vibrating against her as her pussy pulsed. His fingers slid up her legs to her opening. He brushed against her wet pussy, then pushed two fingers in, loving how tight she felt.

"Daniel, take me," Sophia begged.

He lifted and moved up her body. Her heated skin looked rosy with lovemaking. They were skin on skin from their head to their legs. Sophia opened her legs, and he lowered, his cock prodding her opening.

Surprise filled him as she moved fast and pressed up, taking his cock in one quick thrust. Then her legs were behind his back, holding him in place.

The wet heat of her pussy felt like heaven as he started to pump into her. A shiver ripped through him, and he knew he wouldn't last long. It had been a while since he'd had sex, and this woman turned him inside out.

They were connected completely as they gave into all their deepest desires and passions. He lowered and pressed his lips against hers in a kiss that drew out every emotion and drained them into her. Daniel wanted to prove to her just how much she meant to him as their tangled limbs and sweaty bodies moved together in perfect bliss until they both found release in each other's arms.

He never wanted to let this woman go. She meant more than just sex to him. She was the world. Now he just had to find a way to keep her safe.

CHAPTER TWENTY-FOUR

Sophia couldn't believe they'd had sex, and not just sex. That had been more than she'd ever experienced before. They'd transcended what she'd thought love was and had met in a place of perfection. Never before had her body sung like that.

Once she could breathe again, she ran her fingers over his back and through his sweat-dampened hair. He nuzzled her neck, his lips teasing her skin. She moved her head to give him easier access, and he moaned as he kissed his way to her collarbone.

Daniel lifted up on his elbow and stared down into her eyes. She liked how he hadn't shaved for a few days so his whiskers were thicker. When his whiskers had grazed her thighs, she'd loved the feeling. Everything with this man was good.

"You like?"

"I like being with you," Sophia whispered.

"I really like being with you. I'm glad you came back."

Laughter bubbled up and spilled out. "I am, too. I honestly didn't think we would end up here."

He tugged on her earlobe. "Neither did I."

She sighed and lay back against the mattress, trying not to let the worry seep in. Just because she'd been mentioned in a police report didn't mean that Brandon would find her. He may never find her. She could live her whole life here and never see him again.

"What are you thinking?"

She sat up and stared at him, stretched out in her bed—well, the bed she'd been borrowing. She guessed it really was his bed. She brushed her fingers over his shoulder and down to his pec. He was the best-looking guy she'd ever been with. The scar Sherie left didn't look so bad, but it was there, probably reminding him daily how he'd messed up.

"I think that I'm lucky. You are the best thing to happen to me."

Daniel's expression turned serious. "Even though you were attacked by someone from my past."

Sophia nodded. "Yes, even with that. You really are the best thing in my life."

Daniel lifted his eyebrows but said nothing. She drew in a slow breath, wishing she could block her past, but it was always there, sliding in reminders to her thoughts when she least needed them.

"What? I've had a lot of bad stuff happen."

He pulled her close and kissed the top of her head as he hugged her. "I know. I'm going to make sure bad things are a thing of the past."

They lay like that for a while, and then her stomach grumbled. He pulled back and smiled, his eyes twinkling with happiness.

"I'm hungry, too," Daniel said.

She laughed and kissed his shoulder. "It's that obvious, isn't it?"

"Sure. Let's get something."

They stood and kissed, their bodies still humming with desire though they'd just had awesome sex. They moved together as if they had been made for each other. She felt like they were two halves of a whole. A little fear slithered through her thoughts. What if she wasn't enough? What if Daniel figured out he didn't love her?

They were pulling on clothes when Daniel moved closer and pulled her into a kiss. When he finished, he leaned his forehead against hers. "I don't know what that look on your face is about, but you don't have to doubt how much I care about you."

A shiver whipped through her. Finding someone like Daniel while she'd been running from her past had been a shock. Why couldn't she have found him without having to experience the other stuff?

For once, she didn't feel alone or worried about what might happen next. She just basked in the warmth of Daniel's—was this love? It felt more than just friendship and more than just getting off. Maybe what they had was the beginnings of love. Whatever it was, she let herself be completely immersed in every moment with him. It was unlike anything she'd ever known, but it was real, and true, and wonderful.

She stopped by the bathroom, and while she washed her hands, she stared at her reflection. Her lips were swollen, her cheeks rosy. The fear and sadness she'd grown used to seeing in her eyes wasn't there. She actually looked happy.

Her stomach twisted as thoughts of her past hit hard. Could she make this man happy, or was she defective? Sophia pushed away the weirdness that had no part in her relationship with Daniel. They'd known each other for a while, and their attraction had been obvious from the first day. Daniel wasn't Brandon.

She entered the main room and found Daniel working on making their dinner. A shiver snaked through her. Not once had Brandon helped her cook anything.

Daniel flashed her a smile and held up an onion. "Wait," he said as he put the onion back onto the shelf. "Will you kiss me if I have stinky breath?"

Sophia giggled. "If I eat onion, too, neither one of us will notice."

"Whew. I was worried there for a second. I need your kisses."

Her heart felt lighter than it had in a long while. "And I need yours."

She moved closer, and he pulled her to him. She liked how they fit together. He dipped his head and kissed her cheek, then her lips. When he pulled back, he hummed with satisfaction. "You're a good person, Sophia."

She winced. "How do you feel now that you know that's not my real name?"

He shrugged. "Sophia is close enough to Sophie. Are you okay with me calling you Sophia?"

A shiver slid down her back. "Totally okay." She didn't know how she would feel if Daniel called her

Angela or even Sophie. She wanted no part of her past to invade her new life.

"I like Sophia."

She flashed him a smile. "Thanks."

Being with Daniel felt right. Maybe her life wouldn't be perfect, but she had hope for their future. She wanted to believe worry was a thing of her past. She and Daniel were great together, and they could move forward. She could truly say she was happy with how life had worked out.

CHAPTER TWENTY-FIVE

Daniel felt like Sophia had blossomed in the last week. After Sherie had attacked, he'd feared it would set Sophia back, but she seemed happier now.

Sophia had six customers to clean for, including Whitney's B&B, which gave her a steady income. She said she liked the job and didn't mind cleaning other people's houses.

The purchase of his house was coming along. Anne believed the bank would be ready to close in about three weeks. Life seemed to be on a path to awesomeness. He was happy with the nursery, happy with the house, and more than happy with Sophia. She hadn't moved into his place yet, but they were talking about her moving to his place. He figured by the time he was ready to move into his new house,

Sophia would be more than willing to share his bed every night. They'd be more than roommates, and that was perfect for him.

Another snowstorm hit, dusting the mountains with white powder, but temperatures warmed and melted everything. There was a wave of people in town from the city, probably trying to get in the last hike of the year. Zeke and the rest of the guys on the rescue team had to go out again, but thankfully this time the two hikers were still alive.

The order of Christmas trees would come in soon, and he wondered what type of tree Sophia likcd. Last year he hadn't put up a tree in his place because his apartment was just too small, but he had decorated a tree at the nursery.

Frank was scheduled to work this afternoon, and he wanted to surprise Sophia and take her to dinner. The weather was supposed to be great, and he hoped she would agree to spend the night.

A car pulled up into the lot, and four women got out. They weren't locals, or he at least hadn't seen them before.

"Hello, can I help you?"

"We're looking for flowers. The cabin where we're staying doesn't have enough bling factor so we're going to plant some pretty flowers in the front and make it look better."

He'd heard many strange things, but this was one of the weirdest. "So you're staying at a rental cabin, and you're going to plant flowers."

"Of course. We do this sort of thing all the time. Something to make it look more so our fans don't think we went cheap on the rental, though we totally did this time."

He didn't have time to argue or tell them they were crazy for planting flowers at a house they didn't own. He hoped the owner of the cabin didn't get angry, but then again, it wasn't his problem.

He helped them pick out flowers and rang them up, happy to have the customer but worried they were overstepping. It wasn't his place to stick his nose in, and he figured those women could manage their own lives.

One thing that did annoy him was that throughout their shopping experience, they kept snapping photo after photo. He wanted to snap at them, to tell them to grow up and quit acting like they were the center of attention, but he kept his agitation to himself. Maybe he was just annoyed. They weren't harming anyone.

Frank pulled in just as the women left. "Hey, boss, how was today?"

"Good. We just sold out about half our flowers."

"Really? That's good, I guess."

Daniel chuckled. "It does pay the bills. Now I need to figure out if I need to buy more. It's late in the season, but people may want to spruce up their beds when visitors come for the holidays."

"Is that why you sold so many just now?"

Daniel shook his head. "No, there was a group of women renting a cabin who wanted it to look better in photos, so they bought a bunch of flowers."

"Wow."

"Right? I emphasized the no-return policy. They didn't seem to care."

"Tell Sophia I said hi," Frank said as he headed back to the greenhouse.

A smile tugged at Daniel's lips. He liked that his employees had accepted Sophia being here. They didn't know the full story, but it didn't matter.

He checked on a few things in the office, then prepared to leave to pick Sophia up at the house where she was working. Eventually, she would need a vehicle. Cars were expensive, and trucks even more so. She wasn't sure about owning a car, but he wanted her to have independence.

When he turned onto the street where Sophia was cleaning, he saw the women who'd purchased the flowers planting them in the beds. They weren't doing a great job, but it wasn't his business.

Sophia had come outside to wait for him. She shot an annoying glance at the women planting the flowers, rolling her eyes when he stopped the truck to let her in. He helped her put her supplies in the back of the truck, and the women next door burst out laughing as one of them fell over in the dirt.

"They're making a mess of that," Sophia said.

Daniel nodded. "They are. It looks like not one of them has ever planted flowers."

"I almost feel bad enough to stop and help them, but I don't know."

"You're a good person, Sophia."

The women saw him and waved. "Yoo-hoo, we know you," one of them hollered.

"I sold them the flowers," Daniel said in a low voice before he flashed the women a smile and waved. "Have fun," he called out as he let Sophia into the truck, then ran around and hopped in. He wanted to escape before any of the women could ask him for help. The flowers looked awful, with most just sitting on the dirt instead of being planted.

They'd driven about a block before Sophia let go

of the breath she seemed to be holding. He slowed for a stop sign and glanced over at her.

"You okay?"

She rolled her eyes. "That was frustrating. They were barely digging holes for those plants. Some of the holes were only an inch or so deep. They don't know what they are doing. It's frustrating. Also, they spent all afternoon being very loud. I mean, really loud. Yelling about everything from when to schedule waxing appointments to who took the shit in the master bedroom toilet. I swear, if I lived next to them, I'd go crazy."

Daniel burst out laughing. "They were a bit much when they were at the shop. But they bought a lot of plants, and I'm happy about the money I made."

Sophia chuckled. "That's good. So are we heating a pizza or making something else?"

"Neither. I thought we could go out."

"I'm filthy."

"So am I. Let's take a shower."

She glanced at him, her cheeks pink. "Are you just trying to get me naked?"

Daniel grew warm. "Maybe. I like having you naked. But no, you can take your shower first."

"I don't have clothes at your place, do I?" she asked.

"You have that dress and a jacket."

"Oh, I forgot about those. Sure, I'm happy just spending time with you. Even if we're eating sandwiches, I'd be happy."

"You're easy to please. I like that about you. It doesn't mean we're not going out. I just like that you're you."

Sophia's cheeks turned even pinker. She looked good, better than she had when she'd first shown up here. She'd gained some weight, which looked good on her. He was glad he'd been able to help her find some peace. She deserved happiness.

CHAPTER TWENTY-SIX

Daniel had great timing, or maybe he could just read her. After he helped her wash her body, he spun her to face the wall and slid in, going deep on the first thrust. She needed hot, wild sex, and he delivered, making her come twice before he pulled out and came against her back.

They were playing a little too loose with protection, and she knew she needed to find a doctor and make sure the device she'd had implanted was still working. That had been back when she'd turned eighteen and had just started getting serious with Brandon. He had never known she'd gone to the doctor, and she'd been thrilled he never figured it out.

She didn't want to get pregnant, but if something

happened with Daniel, she didn't think it would be a big deal. She wouldn't mind being tied to Daniel for years. He was a good man, and she knew even if they didn't work out, Daniel would be the type of father a child needed.

They dressed quickly and headed to On The Rocks. She liked the place and enjoyed the people who worked there. She felt a sense of contentment and peace that she had never felt before. She knew that it was partially due to the amazing sex they had just had, but there was more to it than just physical desire.

The obnoxious women who had done a disastrous job planting the flowers came in about ten minutes after she and Daniel had been seated.

The volume went up about eighty percent as they laughed loudly and talked even louder. Sophia could tell the regulars were getting annoyed.

"Someone is going to tell them to shut up," Sophia said.

Daniel rolled his eyes. "They are louder than any summer crowd. It's like they've turned the volume up to eleven. I can hardly hear myself think."

Their food arrived, and Sophia took a bite, enjoying the food almost as much as she enjoyed the company.

She'd just loaded up her second bite when the four women noticed them and came over to the table. They were all smiles, but Sophia felt like it was all fake. She'd never understood how to be like these women.

"I don't think we've had the pleasure of being introduced yet, have we? I'm Elle. The one with her phone out is Kim, that little blonde is Katie, and over there is Rachel. We wanted to tell you the place looks amazing with the flowers. Those plants look so good now."

Surprise shifted through Sophia. She was amazed they'd been able to do anything good with the mess they'd created.

"That's great," Sophia said, trying to give a real smile instead of a fake one.

"Good to hear," Daniel added.

The women eyed Daniel, looking him up and down. Sophia wanted to laugh but said nothing. Again she was struck by how little she understood about women like them.

"So is this the only restaurant in town?" one of the women asked.

"There are a few places to eat. This is one of the best. There is a place open for breakfast and a coffee shop. It's a small town," Daniel said.

One of the women laughed. "I wish there was a dance club. I'd love to get my freak on."

Sophia almost burst out laughing but held it in. They chatted for a few more minutes—actually, it was more like the women talked at them before finally returning to their table.

"That was amusing," Sophia said.

"Truly." Daniel shook his head and chuckled.

"So, want to drive by and see what those flowers look like?"

Sophia shot a glance at the women, then nodded. "Oh, yea. I do."

They finished eating and snuck out while the women were chatting up Hank and Zeke. Sophia noticed a few guys entering the restaurant as they were leaving.

"That's interesting," she said as Daniel opened the passenger side door for her.

Daniel huffed out a breath. "Those guys are all single."

Sophia narrowed her gaze at him, wondering what he was saying. Then he winked, and realization dawned.

"Oh—oh!," Sophia said. "And those women seem like partying is a huge part of their lifestyle."

Daniel chuckled. "Some of those guys are going to get some tonight."

Sophia laughed as Daniel shut the door. They drove over to the house where they'd seen the women planting flowers, and both of them were surprised it didn't look too bad.

"That's interesting."

"Yeah, that's not bad," Sophia said.

"Well, I'm glad they made it work. I honestly feared they would try to return them."

Sophia gasped. "People don't do that, do they?"

"You would be surprised what some people think they can get away with."

"I'm sorry. That sucks."

"Are you sleeping at my place tonight?"

She turned to face him, studying his profile. When he slowed for the stop sign, he turned to look at her, his lips spread into a wide smile.

"You're beautiful."

Heat filled her face. "You say stuff like that, and I don't know what to do."

"Just say thank you. So are you going to stay?"

She blew out a breath, faking a sigh. "I guess so." Then she laughed and reached out, squeezing his thigh. "Of course. I enjoy being with you. I just don't want you getting tired of me."

"I won't. I like you a lot, Sophia. I know we're moving fast, but I really like you."

"Good, because I really like you, too."

This was the type of relationship she always wanted but believed wasn't real. She'd read a few books but hadn't believed it would ever be possible to find someone who cared about her as a person and not just someone for sex. Being with Daniel was the happiest she'd ever been, and she couldn't imagine life without him.

CHAPTER TWENTY-SEVEN

Daniel liked having Sophia around. They'd been together for a couple of weeks, which almost seemed unreal. This morning, she'd said she wanted to work at the nursery with him before her cleaning jobs so they could spend time together, even if they were both busy.

The first of the Christmas tree deliveries arrived, and he, Frank, and Will started setting up the trees, making sure they all looked mostly healthy. It was late November and Thanksgiving was the next day. People would be clamoring to get a tree. Most of the stock was good, with only a few trees looking a little worse for wear.

Around lunchtime, he went in search for Sophia,

finding her in the office getting dressed to go clean another house.

"Wow, those trees really smell."

Daniel glanced down at his clothes. "I guess I am covered with their scent."

"It's not bad, just strong."

"What are your plans today?"

"I'm going to clean Mrs. Westings' house, then sit in the coffee shop until you can swing by and pick me up. I thought we could make burgers tonight."

Daniel brushed a kiss over her lips. "Sounds good. I'll see you later. Have a good day."

"I will."

"Oh, do you need me to drive you over?" Daniel asked.

Sophia shook her head, her ponytail swishing from side to side. "I want to walk. The weather is good, and I need the exercise. Plus, you have that delivery coming in, right?"

Daniel checked the time. "Ugh. I do. Thanks for reminding me."

"Any time, sweetie."

He smirked, likening the nicknames they were trying out. "I'll miss you." He planted a kiss on her lips before she left and wished they'd had time to eat lunch together. One thing he never wanted to do was make her feel guilty for having a job. She needed her free time.

The truck was late, and he felt like that was a bad omen. He should have listened to his gut and checked the guy's inventory before he started to unload. After the driver unloaded the first pallet of bags, Daniel glanced into the back of the truck.

"Shit, this isn't our stuff," Daniel called to Frank.

Frank came close and looked. "That's for a restaurant or something."

The driver stopped the forklift and came over, looking angry at them standing in the way. "What's going on?"

"This isn't our stuff," Daniel said.

"Are you sure?" the driver asked as he stared at both Daniel and Frank.

Frank's eyebrows lifted. "Very. It's not our stuff."

"What's on the bill of lading?" Daniel asked.

"Listen," the driver said. "I just deliver the stuff. Are you sure this isn't yours? I hate having to figure this stuff out."

Daniel shrugged. "Well, I can guarantee that we don't need tomato sauce. Who loaded the truck?"

Frank looked at the paperwork the driver had passed him when he arrived. "This isn't for us at all. Those bags were flour."

The driver grabbed the sheets he'd given Frank and groaned. "Shit. I'm sorry. I was wrong. This was wrong. I…crap."

"We'll help you get that loaded up," Frank said.

"I'm going to get into so much trouble," the driver mumbled as he moved to load the pallet of flour.

Daniel looked at the paperwork and shook his head. He couldn't believe they'd received a load destined for a restaurant in Charleston. The restaurant had probably received their truck full of supplies. He could get by, but the restaurant was probably hurting.

After they cleared up the mess and figured out the truck with their things would be there in the morning, Daniel decided to clean out one of the sheds they stored their equipment in and check on the greenhouse.

He enjoyed his job and sometimes got lost in work. Frank stopped by to say goodbye, and Daniel couldn't believe how late it was.

"Bye. Thanks for your hard work today," Daniel called out as Frank waved goodbye. It was odd that Sophia hadn't texted. She should be done cleaning. Maybe she had decided to do something else.

He thought back to what she'd said she would be

doing after she cleaned, and he swore she'd said she would head to the coffee shop and wait for him to pick her up. She knew to text him when she finished. He could have swung by at any time to pick her up.

Daniel called her number, but it went straight to voicemail. Sophia always charged her phone at night and carried a charging cable to her jobs. Maybe she was on the phone with someone. He texted her to call him immediately.

He headed into the office, but something didn't sit right with him. Sophia would have texted or called. She liked being in contact with him.

He pulled up the information about the coffee shop and saw that they'd closed almost an hour ago. Shit, where had the time gone? And where the heck was Sophia?

Without hesitation, he called her again and then again. She would answer him if he called multiple times. He knew it. There was something desperately wrong, and he had no idea how to find her.

CHAPTER TWENTY-EIGHT

Sophia finished cleaning the Westings' house, happy to receive the extra tip Mrs. Westings always left for her. She liked the older couple because they usually made cookies and wanted her to sit and chat with them for a little while before she began cleaning. They treated her like a human, not a servant.

The coffee shop had promoted a new sweet coffee drink for a few weeks, and she was excited to try one of the caramel concoctions. It was a treat she never would have thought about before but was looking forward to today.

She'd walked a few blocks and still had three blocks to go when a white van pulled to the curb in front of her. Her stomach tightened, but she brushed off the fear. Fallport was a small town, not a big city.

Though this looked weird, there was no way it was as strange as it appeared.

The skin at the nape of her neck prickled as she walked past the van, thinking something was very wrong. She felt relief as she moved past the van, and nothing happened. She would chalk this up to being paranoid and laugh about it with Daniel.

A noise sounded behind her, and she turned to look, blinking against the sun as it dipped low behind a line of trees. At first, she couldn't make out the person in the back of the van, but then they spoke, and there was no mistaking who it was.

"Hello, Angela. It's time for me to clip your wings and make sure you never fly away."

Sophia turned to run, but something hit her and dropped her to her knees. She tried to scream, but whatever hit her made it impossible for her to respond.

By the time she could move, she was in the back of the van being driven away. She had no clue how long they drove or where they were headed, but she knew this was it. Brandon wouldn't let her go.

The van made a sharp turn, followed by another quick turn. Sophia rolled around, pain sliding through her as she bumped into something hard. The van stopped, and she reached out, trying to gain some leverage to get up. The sound of a siren grew louder then it quieted.

"Fuck!" Brandon yelled.

Sophia wanted to laugh, but she knew Brandon and had laughed at him before. It hadn't ended well for her.

Brandon cut the engine on the van and stood, moving to the back of the van where she was. Sophia moved to the far end, as far away from him as she could.

"Someone must have turned me in. We're walking." Brandon reached for her, but she slapped his hand away.

He cocked his fist, and she flinched. His laughter made her want to hit him. But she wasn't as strong as he was, and there was no way she could win a fight against him.

"Bitch, you'd better do what I say. Get up, and let's get moving."

She said nothing as she rolled to her hands and knees. He opened the back door of the van, and she stepped out. They were on a dirt road that had trees growing all around it.

He handcuffed her wrists in front of her and pushed her shoulder. "Walk."

"Where?" She hated how much her voice shook. Brandon was evil, and she hated him.

He pushed her back, almost knocking her to the ground. "Through the woods, dumbass. Where else do you think we're going."

"There's no way we'll make it. Do you even know where you're going?"

"Shut up."

She didn't want to go out into the woods with him. Brandon was the type of guy who acted like he knew what he was doing but rarely did. He talked a big game, but he didn't know anything. She would trust Daniel to guide her out here but going out into the woods with Brandon meant sure death. He wouldn't be able to make it to another town, much less back in the direction they'd come from.

Worry filled her. They had no supplies, no water, and no food. She had her jacket but didn't have gloves or proper boots. Her tennis shoes were better than flats or heels, but she needed hiking boots out here. No question, they weren't going to be able to do this.

Deep shadows filled the dense forest, and she stumbled more than she walked. Sophia struggled to keep up with Brandon, her feet slipping on dirt that had turned to mud from the rains and recent snow.

Snow still clung to the land in a few of the deep-shadowed areas. That wasn't a good sign.

"We're going to get lost, and it's cold."

Brandon turned to face her, anger flashing in his eyes. "Shut up, bitch. I told you to shut up, now do as your told." His hand flew, slamming into her cheek. She stumbled and fell against a tree. She couldn't do this again. She wouldn't move from this spot.

Brandon started walking again, but she wasn't going to go. Maybe she could find her way back to the van and then make her way into town. She wasn't sure which way to go on the road.

"Move," Brandon said.

"No."

He stalked back, his movements exaggerated. His hand came up and fisted her hair, tugging her closer. She could smell the cigarette trying to cover his bad breath.

"Walk!" His face had twisted into a mask of hatred, and how he pulled her hair hurt.

She wanted to tell him to go to hell, but she started moving, knowing she would have to find a way to escape him. He didn't care about her well-being or even his, for that matter. He was a dumbass who thought he could find his way out of this forest, and she knew he couldn't.

The sun was sinking so fast she knew they would be trapped out here all night. At least Mrs. Westings had fed her finger sandwiches and cookies. She wasn't starving, but they would need water soon. Maybe she could take some of the snow. That would at least give her a little moisture.

"Move faster," Brandon barked.

Sophia moved behind him, watching the ground as best she could in the fading light. Brandon wasn't paying attention and stepped out of the tree line, then scrambled back fast. She froze, seeing that Brandon had almost stepped off a cliff. She wished he had. Maybe it was wrong to wish death on him, but he deserved nothing less.

"You're laughing, aren't you?"

She shook her head, knowing that nothing she said could convince him otherwise when he got this way. "I wasn't laughing."

"I can see it in your eyes."

Sophia backed away, but he grabbed her arm and tugged her close. She screamed and tried to turn, but Brandon pulled her toward the edge.

"No!" she cried out as she struggled against him, trying to break free from his grip on her arms. But he just laughed at her and pushed her to the edge.

The fear running through her was sharp as a

knife, and she gasped for breath. If he let go and pushed her just a little, she would plummet to the ground far below. The drop was about fifty feet, maybe more, to the rocks below.

Terror clawed at her, leaving her gasping for air. She latched onto his arm, holding tight, praying he didn't push her. The bastard cackled as he shook his arm, pretending to push her.

She thought about calling out for help, but the words stuck in her throat. Tears filled her eyes. She wanted to tell Daniel she loved him. They'd hinted at the idea but not said those words. Now, this psychopath was trying to kill her.

He pulled her back, and she dropped to the ground, crawling away from the edge as he threw back his head and laughed. They were deep in the woods, far from the town of Fallport so he could laugh at her as loudly as he wanted, and no one would come for her. She had little doubt someone would see them as he led her deeper into the woods and to her death.

Sophia closed her eyes, trying to block out the pain in her body and the terror that filled her soul. This was it—there would be no escape from Brandon and his twisted plans. She just had to put one foot in front of the other until the very end came for her. What had she ever seen in him? The man was evil. She'd been too scared to leave, thinking no one would love her. She'd never even considered being alone was a better option, but it would have been.

She wished she could go back to the woman she'd been before and tell her she was worth so much more than the crap Brandon was putting her through. What she had with him had never been love. Sure, she felt something for him, but it had never been love. There wasn't a way to have love for a man that beat her. It was false, like a false god or false hope. Whatever they'd shared had never been real. If only she had realized it then.

Brandon forced her to her feet and made her walk until darkness fell over the forest. Her panic grew as she huddled against the rocks, hoping Daniel knew she was missing. What if he didn't care? She knew better than to think that but being with Brandon again was doing a number on her mind.

CHAPTER TWENTY-NINE

Daniel headed into town to search for Sophia. A weird feeling twisted through him and was exacerbated when a patrol car screamed past him.

He slowed, then sped up and headed to Zeke's place. He had just pulled into a parking space when he heard another siren.

Zeke stepped out, his eyes narrowed, making him almost look sinister. Daniel stepped out of his truck and moved to Zeke, determined to find out what was happening.

"Do you know what that's about?"

Zeke glanced around and then moved them away from the door to the bar. "Someone called in an abduction."

Daniel's head started to pound, and his stomach

turned. If he'd eaten recently, he was sure he would have vomited everything right then.

He gripped Zeke's arm, panic ping-ponging inside. "I can't get ahold of Sophia."

Zeke's lips turned down even more. "Call her again."

Daniel pulled out his phone and called. "No answer. Straight to voicemail."

"Send another text."

He typed out the words begging Sophia to call him. The weight of the situation made his whole body ache. Had Brandon caught up with her? She'd been so careful. But then he'd had her report Sherie's assault to the police. Guilt thicker than mud filled him.

"Fuck. This is my fault."

Zeke shot him a look and frowned. "How is this your fault?"

"I had her report that assault from Sherie. She'd said she didn't want to have her name on a report."

Zeke shook his head. "You don't know that's what happened. Come on. Let's head to the station and see what Simon has to say."

"Fuck, Zeke, tomorrow is Thanksgiving."

Zeke nodded. "I know. We'll find her. Give me your keys, and I'll drive us over."

Daniel usually didn't hand his keys over to just anyone, but this was Zeke. "Do you think this is about Sophia?"

Zeke backed out of the space and did a U-turn since the streets were dead. "No clue, but we're going to find out."

They were at the station in no time. Daniel pocketed his keys when Zeke handed them over. They stepped into the station, and relief spread over Simon Hill's face when he saw Zeke.

"Are they in the mountains?"

"We aren't sure yet. What we know is the call came in around five." Simon pointed to one of the residential streets on the map.

Guilt filled Daniel. He should have told Sophia to wait at the Westings' house. He could have taken a few minutes from work and picked her up.

"They said it was a white van. The woman screamed and fought, but she was no match. We're not sure who—"

"It's Sophia," Daniel said.

Simon turned to him, his eyes narrowed. Daniel had helped Simon pick out new bushes for the front of his house. They'd spent some time talking last summer, but that was friendly and at Daniel's nursery. This was here on Simon's turf, and Sophia was missing, maybe dead by now.

"Who?" Simon asked.

"Sophia. She came here the first week of October. She's been living at the nursery's office and started cleaning people's homes. She was working at the Westings' house today. That's why she was there. She cleaned for them. Then she planned to walk to the coffee shop to wait until I could pick her up. She must have been running late. Usually, she finishes the Westings' place closer to four."

"What do you know about this woman?" Simon asked.

"Her ex was abusive. She ran to escape his abuse. She goes by Sophia though her name is Angela Sophie McDonald." Daniel glanced up and met Simon's gaze. "If he has her, she might be dead by now." The words felt like glass in his mouth, but they had to be said. The police needed to know who they were going after.

A call came in, reporting that someone saw the van on the eastern side of the city, closer to one of the roads where hikers liked to park in the summer to pick up one of the trails.

Daniel met Zeke's gaze. "What are her chances of surviving out there tonight?"

Zeke pulled out his phone and looked at one of his weather applications. "It's not going to dip below fifty-five tonight here in Fallport, so a little cooler in the mountains. No snow until tomorrow night. We need to find her before noon tomorrow when the weather changes with that front moving through."

The weight of Zeke's words made Daniel's stomach pull tight. He hated that Sophia had been taken by Brandon. They weren't sure it was him, but Daniel knew the only person who would come after her was her ex.

They stared at the map, none of them saying anything as desperation thickened. This wasn't the time to get lost in the woods, not with a cold front sweeping in.

"I need to get her information to the Feds," Simon said. "We need to make sure they can't hop on a plane."

Simon left the area and headed into one of the offices. Zeke picked up the police radio and turned up the volume. Since they'd arrived, few updates had come over the device, but he knew they would update once they had something.

A few minutes after Simon stepped into his office, the radio lit up. They'd found a white van on one of the dirt roads where hikers liked to park. It was about fifty feet away from the main road, and they'd been lucky they'd found it.

Daniel glanced outside, realizing it was pitch black. They'd found the van, but the officers wouldn't go far into the woods at this time. They'd end up lost.

Simon came out of his office, his expression tight. "Zeke, how many of your guys are in town?"

Zeke's lips turned down as his frown deepened. "Four. The rest are scattered because of the holiday."

"I can go out with you," Daniel said.

Simon shot his gaze Daniel's way, then shook his head. "I don't know."

"Listen, time is of the essence. The storm is coming this way, and her ex is volatile. She doesn't have time for us to wait on another team coming in here, not today. Thanksgiving day starts in a few hours, which means people are with their families. We have five guys who can go into the forest and track them."

Simon turned his gaze on Zeke. "It's your call."

Zeke turned to Daniel and studied him. "I know you're upset. Can you keep your emotions in check?"

"I'll do whatever you need. I'm stable."

"If we don't find her alive, are you willing to listen to orders?"

Daniel nodded. He wanted to find her alive and well, and if he couldn't find her well, he just wanted her alive. "I'm good with it. I won't do something stupid."

"Okay, let's get the ball rolling. I need to grab my supplies. Daniel, where are your things?"

"At my apartment. I'll catch up with you here."

Zeke turned back to Simon. "I'll call in the guys, and we'll head out."

"Sounds good. I'll see you in a few."

Daniel dropped Zeke at the bar so he could pick up his truck. He had his bag packed, ready to go if called up. It had been a while since he'd been tagged to go out and help them find someone, but he was always ready. Anger and fear twisted through him. Sophia was too important to lose.

She'd just found happiness, too. Her life had been tough, and she'd put up with so much crap from Brandon and her brother. It wasn't fair that one person had to go through so much. She deserved happiness.

Tears threatened as his emotions kicked in. He would make sure their life was filled with good things once they got her back. If they found her. If they didn't find her, he would make sure her ex paid dearly.

CHAPTER THIRTY

Sophia felt the kick to her leg as she tried to pry her eyes open. A chill had seeped in overnight, making her bones ache. As she moved and cracked one eyelid open, pain filled her. She felt like someone had run over her with a truck or maybe a steam-roller. Why did she feel so bad? Then it hit, and she remembered Brandon. Fear took over, and she flinched as her eyes flashed open.

He stood above her, not looking so good. "Get up. We need to find a town today."

Her muscles screamed as she moved to stand. Her leg gave out, and she dropped back to kneeling. She tried again, surprised how a half day of hiking had filled her with so much pain. It wasn't just the hiking, though. She'd rolled around in the back of that van, and her ex had hit her, too.

Once on her feet, she tried to stretch, but the cuffs still held her wrists together. "I need to pee."

"Fuck, you are such a needy bitch."

She wanted to tell him to fuck off. He knew she had to pee. They'd need water soon, too. She wouldn't survive long if the weather got colder. The jacket she had was just barely enough for last night. She considered herself lucky that Brandon had allowed her to keep it. Then again, he may not have even thought of taking her jacket.

After she finished and pulled her pants back up, even though it was extremely difficult with her hands cuffed, she turned to watch him. What did he have planned for today? He wasn't the type of guy to think long-term. She doubted he knew where the next trailhead near a town was located. They weren't going to survive unless she forced them back to safety.

"Hurry up. Let's move out. I'm hungry," Brandon said.

Sophia kept her lips sealed and didn't rub in the fact that he should have thought of food before abducting her. If she'd had time to plan this, she would have a pack full of food and water or those tablets that made river water mostly safe to drink. He'd screwed up, and she didn't think Brandon was mature enough to own up to his mistakes.

They took off at a slower pace. Sophia saw some snow a few feet off the trail and moved toward it. Brandon's anger rose, and he rushed her but didn't hit her.

"What are you doing?"

"We need water."

Sophia moved to the snow and bent, shivering as the cold intensified. If the weather turned at all, they would die. She got two mouthfuls of snow before Brandon shoved her away. He ate more snow than she had, but she was fine. The snow had been making her cold, and all she wanted was a nice warm fire without Brandon's drama.

She could imagine sitting next to Daniel with a fire crackling in their fireplace, hot cocoa in a mug on the table, and snacks ready for them to eat. Her stomach grumbled, and she had to force the thoughts of food from her mind.

Brandon stood and swiped the back of his hand over his mouth. "We need to make good time. Which way do we go?"

Her mouth dropped open as she stared at him.

He had no clue where to go. He would probably hit her for this.

She shrugged. "I don't know." Though she'd spent some time in the woods when she'd first arrived, she didn't know where they were now.

"You live here, shouldn't you know?"

"I live down there, not here. All the trees look the same." That wasn't quite the truth, but it was close enough that he wouldn't know she was lying. She probably could figure out how to get them back to Fallport if she had a compass and time. But she had neither.

"Fuck!" Brandon yelled.

She winced but realized the more he yelled, the better the chance someone would find them. She didn't know how to make him yell, though. Before she left, her just existing seemed to have pissed him off. He hadn't really hit her this morning. He must be off his game.

For a moment, she thought about needling him to get him to yell, but she didn't want to get hit again. She pointed him in a direction and hoped he didn't realize they were circling back the way they'd come.

She said little for the first hour they spent walking. Brandon seemed to be happy to follow her lead.

Not that she knew where they were going, but she was headed in the general direction of Fallport.

They stopped for Brandon to take a piss, and she relieved herself, too. She spied another white patch of snow and moved to it, picking off some of the tree debris before scooping up a little snow and eating it.

Brandon came over and grabbed some snow, this time without pushing her out of the way. There'd been flashes of him being kind in the past, but they were quickly followed by outbursts. He couldn't be nice long enough for her to forget how hard his punches were and how mean he could turn. After meeting Daniel and seeing him in all sorts of situations, she could never forgive Brandon. She never should have forgiven him after the first blow, but she'd thought it had been her fault.

It was weird how women were taught men couldn't handle their emotions. That was the crux of the message that men and other women couched in messages blaming women for how men behaved. Really, it was like they were ticking time bombs that couldn't take one ounce of pressure. She'd gone from thinking men were all powerful and deserved to be waited on hand and foot to realizing that a real man wouldn't freak out and hit a woman just because he didn't get his way or his food was a few minutes late. A real man would help in the kitchen and help with the laundry. She'd seen that with Daniel, though she didn't live full-time with him. He'd always been willing to help her switch clothes to the dryer or clean the kitchen. She'd even come out of the shower to find him cooking dinner for them. In all the years she'd been with Brandon, she wasn't sure he ever once turned on the oven.

"How did you find me?" she asked as they started walking again.

"It was easy. You were in a photo on social media. I kept doing image searches, and boom, there you were. The dumb bitch had posted the name and location of where she'd been staying. Then it was easy to get a flight out here and look."

Sophia wanted to tell Brandon to go to hell. She had no idea why he wanted her back in his life. It wasn't like they were friends or anything. Surely he could find someone else to torture.

The forest had been getting lighter as the sun rose. Hunger hit, and the thought of coffee almost made her cry. If she was home with Daniel, she would wake up to the scent of him brewing coffee for them both. She could see it now, him walking around in his shorts or a pair of sweats as he grabbed a mug for her. Sometimes he wore a T-shirt in the morning. Other times he went bare-chested. She loved how soft the hair on his chest was. She missed him so much.

She couldn't go back with Brandon. She had no clue what he had planned for her, but it wouldn't be good.

"Where are we going?"

Sophia looked up. Did he see something that made him think she was backtracking? "To a town."

Brandon moved fast and slammed her against a tree. "Don't make me hurt you, Angela. I don't want to hurt you. I just want you under my thumb. You know how much better you will be when you belong to me? You're nothing without me."

Tears built as pain sizzled down her back to her legs. Exhaustion still lingered from the day before, and hunger had built steam and had the potential to run over her. Tears fell and streamed down her face as the reality of their situation sank in. This was it—there would be no escape now.

Anger rose, and she shoved at his chest. Shock filled his face, so she shoved again. "Leave me alone!" Sophia shouted.

Brandon looked like she'd just taken away his favorite toy or something. His face turned red as his cheeks blew out like a pouting toddler. Maybe she shouldn't have shoved him, but she was tired of his shit. She didn't want to live if it meant she would be his slave again.

He drew his fist back to punch her. She ducked under his arm and ran. She had escaped his anger for a second, but he'd turned around and began chasing her. He had one big advantage—actually, two. His legs were longer, and his hands weren't cuffed. She raced around another tree, moving so he couldn't grab her.

He skidded on the dirt and went down on one knee, giving her time to get farther away. She hopped over a log and ran, but Brandon was faster and blocked her escape. She skidded to a stop before she ran into him.

"You're going to regret doing that," Brandon warned before he threw a punch.

Sophia felt like her soul had left her body as she fell to the ground. She lay crumpled on the forest floor. He'd broken her. Defeated, she blinked up at him, wishing her mind would clear. The anger and hate she saw in his face made her think he might just kill her right there.

His ego and possessiveness had ultimately led them straight into disaster. They were lost in the forest with no supplies, and they were holding a grudge match she was sure to fail.

"You deserve all the hell I'm throwing your way," Brandon said through gritted teeth. He moved to her side and kicked her in the ribs. She cried out and swiveled around, trying to avoid his next kick.

He'd moved so far that his back was to a log about his knee height. Sophia realized the position she had him in, and when he lunged at her, she used her leverage and swung around, pulling her legs tight to her body before kicking out, hitting Brandon in the upper chest.

For a short second, maybe two seconds, she thought her plan hadn't worked. Brandon still looked down at her, but the shock on his face turned priceless as he took a step back to regain his balance, but he had nowhere to go. The log caught him at the back of the knee, keeping his feet and lower legs in place while his ass moved back. The weight of his torso pulled him over, and he fell.

A loud thump, something like a melon hitting the ground, sounded from the other side of the tree. She couldn't see anything but his feet in the air, but they weren't moving.

Sophia tried to sit up, but the pain kept her down. Eventually, she rolled to her side, praying

Brandon wasn't struggling to get up. She needed him to stay down, so she had a chance of getting away.

It took her almost a full minute to stand and then more time to shuffle over to the log and look at Brandon. She could see his chest rising and falling, so he wasn't dead, but he'd been knocked unconscious.

Sophia snorted at the comedy of the situation. In all her years of taking his abuse, she'd never once been able to render him unconscious. Pride slid through her, and her lips wobbled into a small smile. But the battle wasn't over. He could wake up. She had no clue where she was and hoped someone was out there looking for her.

She turned around and took a step, but her legs gave out, and she dropped to her knees. Maybe she could crawl home. She would try walking in a bit, but the abuse Brandon had dished out mixed with exhaustion, and she felt like she was trying to walk through a vat of thick mud. Her legs wouldn't carry her, and her head swam with muddled thoughts.

Daniel had told her about the rescue team. Maybe they knew she'd been taken. But what clues could have been left? She could easily die before they found her. At least she wouldn't die a prisoner to Brandon.

CHAPTER THIRTY-ONE

Daniel hated how long it was taking them to get ready to go out and search for Sophia. She'd spend most of the night in the cold. Fear for her safety ate at him.

He understood their need to ensure they were going out well-equipped. Since this wasn't just two hikers lost in the forest, they had to take precautions. They didn't know if Brandon had weapons or not. He was dangerous, that they knew.

"You ready?" Talon asked?.

Daniel nodded. "I am."

"We're heading out in a few minutes."

Daniel nodded. "Raid, Talon, Brock, and Zeke had stayed in town. The rest were taking vacations to see family or just to get away. He understood, but he wished they were all here with Sophia's life on the line.

He was glad they were allowing him to go with them. He would be very upset if he had to stay here and wait for news.

"We're headed out," Zeke said.

They moved out to the vehicles and loaded up. They were driving to the location where the van had been found. Simon Hill had been happy to let the Eagle Point Search and Rescue Team head out to find Sophia and Brandon. They knew they were heading into danger, which wasn't ideal, but they'd agreed to call in backup if everything went south.

By the time they parked next to the van, the moon was already lowering. That meant the sun would be up soon.

"Keep your radios on eight," Zeke said as they began their trek into the dark forest.

Duke had picked up a scent, moving slower than during the day. Daniel felt relief. Maybe that's what it was. He was happy they were moving now. The sun would be up in a few hours, making searching easier.

He prayed Sophia wasn't dead. If she was, Brandon would never rest because Daniel would find him and torture the hell out of him. He'd never been the type to want to torture someone, but now, he wanted to make Brandon pay.

They paused close to sunrise as Duke found a spot he really liked. Daniel moved closer to the dog and shined his flashlight on the ground.

"I see prints," Zeke said.

Talon nodded. "They were here. Now we just need to figure out where they went next."

Daniel blew out a breath as the guys consulted their maps. Worry made his head ache. He wanted to find Sophia and make sure she was okay. He had started to bargain with God. If they found her, he would give her up if that's what she wanted.

"I think Duke has a good scent," Raid said.

Zeke folded the map. "I agree. I think he's onto something. He's leading us on a good path. I don't want to try another trail, thinking we can outsmart him."

Raid chuckled. "Duke is smarter on this kind of stuff than we'll ever be."

"Ain't that the truth," Talon added.

Brock stood from where he knelt. "Looks like one of them pissed over here. They seemed to have consumed some of the snow over there."

"At least they have some water," Daniel said.

"We need to drink, then let's head out," Zeke said.

They all took sips of their water before Raid sent Duke off to continue following the scent.

He felt lucky he knew the men on the search and rescue team. Only Zeke knew Sophia, but they all were taking this seriously. Not that they didn't take other rescues as seriously, but he liked the raw determination he saw in their expressions. They would find Sophia.

Duke's barking increased in pitch like excitement had him. Daniel felt like they were close to finding something. He picked up his pace, and after cresting a rise, he saw Duke about twenty feet down the slope barking as he stood over something. It took a moment for Daniel to recognize that Duke was standing over a person.

Worry hit hard when he didn't see the person move. He'd worried that Sophia might die, but with Duke making all the ruckus over the person lying still, fear almost brought him to his knees.

Then he saw the person lift a hand to touch the dog. Relief poured through him like a waterfall crashing on the rocks below. Again he almost dropped to his knees, this time because of happiness.

"Anyone see the guy?" Brock asked.

"No," went up from the group as they kept their head on a swivel.

"I've got Sophia," Daniel said, freeing them to search for the guy who had taken her.

Daniel was on his knees, his eyes devouring her features, searching for any trauma. She blinked open her eyes, a smile slowly settling on her lips. She was about to say something when Zeke shouted that he had the jerk.

"Hey," Daniel said after the excitement of finding the other person died down.

Sophia opened her mouth to say something, but only a croak came out. He grabbed the bottle of water and twisted the cap off.

"Can you sit up?"

Sophia nodded as she wiggled to her side and pushed up. He noticed the cuffs on her wrists and helped her to sit up. He moved so she could lean against him as he helped her drink. After she took a few sips, she cleared her throat.

"You came." Her voice was harsh, croaky, but the best sound he'd heard in ages.

"Sophia, of course I came looking for you."

Zeke came close, kneeling in front of them. "Hey, how are you?"

Sophia nodded. "Okay. Brandon dragged me into his van, then took me out here."

"Do you have handcuff keys?" Daniel asked.

Zeke reached into one of the pockets of his pants. "Actually, I do." Zeke moved close to remove the cuffs from Sophia's wrists. "Better?"

"Much better," Sophia said. "Thank you all for not giving up on me."

"We don't know the meaning of giving up. I'm glad you are okay, or will be okay," Zeke said.

"Do you think you can walk?"

Sophia nodded. "I think so. I'm so hungry."

Daniel chuckled. "We brought snacks."

"Oh, thank God." Sophia sat up more, supporting her own weight.

Daniel moved into action, taking out supplies to treat her wounds. Duke came over and sniffed her hand, then sat facing them.

Sophia smiled. "I guess the dog is to thank."

"Duke worked hard," Raid said. "I'm Raid, by the way."

"Thank you for searching for me. I really thought I wasn't going to make it."

"We need to head back soon. A storm is moving in. I'm Brock, and the other two are Zeke and Talon."

Sophia nodded. "Thank you all. You saved me."

"Can you walk?" Brock asked.

She nodded, then looked up. "I'll be fine."

"I'm not fine. She attacked me," Brandon said. "I was minding my own—"

Daniel wanted to jump up and beat the guy until he shut up, but Zeke reached out and slapped him on the head. "Shut up. We know you abducted her. There were witnesses."

"But I'm hurt."

"Well, that's your fault for picking on a badass woman," Zeke said.

Daniel liked the smile on Sophia's face. She had survived. He finished treating the worst of her cuts, and they began their hike back to town. Raid had sent their location back to the police as they traveled so two cops met them about a mile from where they had begun their journey, which also happened to be where the van was parked.

Sophia still needed to be seen by a doctor, but she was safe at home. He'd had things to be thankful for, but never had he been this grateful for anything in his life. Maybe it was too early for them to commit to being together forever, but he was ready. He wanted to let her know just how much he cared for her and how much he wanted her to be a part of his every day.

CHAPTER THIRTY-TWO

Sophia spent the week recovering. She officially moved in with Daniel. He'd closed on the house, and it was a great place to live. They were working on plans for the huge backyard.

After a week of recovering, she was ready to get back to life. She found a used car that Daniel and his friends checked out, making sure it would at least get her around town. That made her cleaning job easier.

Daniel had asked if she wanted to work at the nursery, and she agreed to work when her cleaning schedule allowed her to, but she really liked helping people in Fallport. She had gained a handful of older clients who needed special help. Then she had people calling her because they'd heard about how she'd helped Honey conquer the piles of papers and other things her sister had collected. She found her life rewarding in a way she'd never thought possible.

The police stopped by and assured her Brandon would stay locked up. Turned out he'd killed his boss before he'd come looking for her. He was in a load of trouble that it didn't look like he could escape.

Sophia finished with her cleaning client and headed home, glad to see Daniel's truck in the driveway. She parked behind him and headed in, excited to find out what they were eating for dinner.

"Honey, I'm home."

"I'm in the bedroom," Daniel called out.

She stepped into the bedroom and found Daniel lying on the bed, his hands behind his head. Water flecked the hair on his chest, and she could smell the clean scent of his soap.

"Hey, sexy," she said as she pulled off her shirt and tossed it on the floor.

"Oh, I like this," Daniel said.

"Do you want me to start something for dinner?"

He shook his head. "We can order pizza."

"Awesome," she said as she kicked off her shoes and pulled her socks off.

"First, I want you."

"I need to shower."

Daniel's smile spread wide. "I can get into that."

She laughed as he stood in one fluid motion and was by her side in seconds. "I'm filthy. I had to crawl under Mr. Bromley's bed and retrieve a cat."

"I didn't know he had a cat."

"Neither did he."

Daniel threw back his head, and laughter spilled out, making her feel happier than she'd ever been before.

"I'll have to ask him about his cat the next time I see him."

She shook her head. "I'm not sure he'll keep it."

Daniel led her to the bathroom and turned on the water, getting it to the right temperature. He soaped up her body and washed her hair before he turned her around and slid his hands over her belly, then lower, taking her to heaven.

When she cried out his name, his chuckle vibrated against her neck. She still pulsed with her orgasm when he flipped off the water and grabbed a towel, drying her body. Once they were both out of the shower, he picked her up, carried her into the bedroom, and gently laid her on the clean sheets.

His tongue explored, and his lips teased as he brought her to the edge. When he slid in, she arched up to meet him. They were perfect together. Daniel had brought her into his life, offering comfort and empathy in a way no one else ever had. She felt overwhelmed by his kindness, so vulnerable and exposed in a way that left her terrified and strangely hopeful at the same time. But with those new feelings that scared her a little was an assurance that Daniel would always be there for her, treating her like a partner.

He lifted up, his eyes searching hers. "Sophia, I love you more than I've ever loved anyone."

"I love you, too."

He brushed his lips over hers and then lifted again. "Soon, we're going to discuss marriage because we both know we belong together."

She brushed her fingertips over his cheek as tears filled her eyes. When this man made her cry, it was because of his sweet tenderness and love. She could barely breathe, so great was the swell of love inside.

Daniel captured her hand and kissed each finger, mirroring her emotions in his eyes. Their bodies melted into one—his chest against her breasts, their hips aligned. His heart pulsed against hers, and she knew she would never let him go.

"Forever, my love," Sophia whispered because even without a marriage certificate, she had already committed to being with him for the rest of her life.

231

THE END

OTHER BOOKS BY JULIA BRIGHT

Mountain Rescue

Searching for Sophie

Finding Home

Jenna's SEAL

Ashley's SEAL

Becky's SEAL

Sunshine's SEAL

Audrey's SEAL

Rosalind's SEAL

Fighting for Home

A SEAL for Candace

A SEAL for Deb

A SEAL for Elise

A SEAL for Trixie

A SEAL for Raven

A SEAL for Liz

Special Forces: Operation Alpha

Saving Lorelei

Rescuing Amy

Saving Sloan

Seeking Justice

Justice for Amber

Searching for Keeley

Justice for Oswin

Safety for Eve

Dark Eagle Series

Survive The Fall

Live Past The Edge

Hold on Through the Pain

Endure the Darkness

Storm Corp Series

Determined

Standalone Romance

Acting The Part

All Business

Just One Taste

Unseen Cruelty

ABOUT THE AUTHOR

Julia Bright is the author of the contemporary military romance Dark Eagle series and is an Operation Alpha Author. Julia lives in the south where "bless your heart" is an insult and "shut up" shows love. Julia has been reading since they could open a book and has taken the passion for words and combined it with the love of travel to create stories full of passion and excitement. If you love a good book with a fantastic happily ever after, you'll enjoy a Julia Bright novel. For a dash of paranormal romance and urban fantasy, pick up a book from Julia's USA Today Bestselling JS Bright pen name

facebook.com/AuthorJuliaBright
amazon.com/Julia-Bright/e
bookbub.com/authors/julia-bright

There are many more books in this fan fiction world than listed here, for an up-to-date list go to www.AcesPress.com

You can also visit our Amazon page at:
http://www.amazon.com/author/operationalpha

Special Forces: Operation Alpha World

Christie Adams: Charity's Heart

Linzi Baxter: Dangerous Rescue

Misha Blake: Flash

Anna Blakely: Rescuing Gracelynn

Julia Bright: Saving Lorelei

Cara Carnes: Protecting Mari

Kendra Mei Chailyn: Beast

Melissa Kay Clarke: Rescuing Annabeth

Samantha A. Cole: Handling Haven

Lorelei Confer: Protecting Sara

KaLyn Cooper: Spring Unveiled

Janie Crouch: Storm

Jordan Dane: Redemption for Avery

Tarina Deaton: Found in the Lost

Riley Edwards: Protecting Olivia

Dorothy Ewels: Knight's Queen

Lila Ferrari: Protecting Joy

Nicole Flockton: Protecting Maria

Hope Ford: Rescuing Karina
Amy Gamet: Guarded by the SEAL
Desiree Holt: Protecting Maddie
Jesse Jacobson: Protecting Honor
Rayne Lewis: Justice for Mary
Ireland Lorelei: The Detective
Kristin Lynn: Worth the Risk
Callie Love & Ann Omasta: Hawaii Hottie
JM Madden: Rescuing Olivia
A.M. Mahler: Griffin
Ellie Masters: Sybil's Protector
Trish McCallan: Hero Under Fire
Rachel McNeely: The SEAL's Surprise Baby
KD Michaels: Saving Laura
Olivia Michaels: Protecting Harper
Annie Miller: Securing Willow
Keira Montclair: Wolf and the Wild Scots
MJ Nightingale: Protecting Beauty
Melinda Owens: Betraying Katie
Victoria Paige: Reclaiming Izabel
Danielle Pays: Defending Sarina
Lainey Reese: Protecting New York
KeKe Renée: Protecting Bria
TL Reeve and Michele Ryan: Extracting Mateo
Deanna L. Rowley: Saving Veronica
Angela Rush: Charlotte

Rose Smith: Saving Satin
Tyler Anne Snell: Cowboy Heat
Lynne St. James: SEAL's Spitfire
Discovering Tyler: E.M. Shue
Sarah Stone: Shielding Grace
Jen Talty: Burning Desire
Reina Torres, Rescuing Hi'ilani
LJ Vickery: Circus Comes to Town
R. C. Wynne: Shadows Renewed

Delta Team Three Series

Lori Ryan: Nori's Delta
Becca Jameson: Destiny's Delta
Lynne St James, Gwen's Delta
Elle James: Ivy's Delta
Riley Edwards: Hope's Delta

Police and Fire: Operation Alpha World

Freya Barker: Burning for Autumn
B.P. Beth: Scott
Jane Blythe: Salvaging Marigold
Julia Bright, Justice for Amber
Hadley Finn: Exton
Emily Gray: Shelter for Allegra
Deanndra Hall: Shelter for Sharla
Jenna Harte: Dead But Not Forgotten

India Kells: Shadow Killer
Amber Kuhlman: Protecting Paisley
Reina Torres: Justice for Sloane
Aubree Valentine, Justice for Danielle
Maddie Wade: Finding English

Tarpley VFD Series

Silver James, Fighting for Elena
Deanndra Hall, Fighting for Carly
Haven Rose, Fighting for Calliope
MJ Nightingale, Fighting for Jemma
TL Reeve, Fighting for Brittney
Nicole Flockton, Fighting for Nadia

As you know, this book included at least one character from Susan Stoker's books. To check out more, see below.

SEAL Team Hawaii Series

Finding Elodie

Finding Lexie

Finding Kenna

Finding Monica

Finding Carly

Finding Ashlyn (Feb 2023)

Finding Jodelle (July 2023)

Eagle Point Search & Rescue

Searching for Lilly

Searching for Elsie

Searching for Bristol

Searching for Caryn (April 2023)

Searching for Finley (Sept 2023)

Searching for Heather (TBA)

Searching for Khloe (TBA)

The Refuge Series

Deserving Alaska

Deserving Henley

Deserving Reese (May 2023)
Deserving Cora (Nov 2023)
Deserving Lara (TBA)
Deserving Maisy (TBA)
Deserving Ryleigh (TBA)

Delta Team Two Series

Shielding Gillian
Shielding Kinley
Shielding Aspen
Shielding Jayme (novella)
Shielding Riley
Shielding Devyn
Shielding Ember
Shielding Sierra

SEAL of Protection: Legacy Series

Securing Caite (FREE!)
Securing Brenae (novella)
Securing Sidney
Securing Piper
Securing Zoey
Securing Avery
Securing Kalee
Securing Jane

Delta Force Heroes Series

Rescuing Rayne (FREE!)
Rescuing Aimee (novella)
Rescuing Emily
Rescuing Harley
Marrying Emily (novella)
Rescuing Kassie
Rescuing Bryn
Rescuing Casey
Rescuing Sadie (novella)
Rescuing Wendy
Rescuing Mary
Rescuing Macie (novella)
Rescuing Annie

Badge of Honor: Texas Heroes Series

Justice for Mackenzie (FREE!)
Justice for Mickie
Justice for Corrie
Justice for Laine (novella)
Shelter for Elizabeth
Justice for Boone
Shelter for Adeline
Shelter for Sophie
Justice for Erin
Justice for Milena

Shelter for Blythe
Justice for Hope
Shelter for Quinn
Shelter for Koren
Shelter for Penelope

SEAL of Protection Series

Protecting Caroline (FREE!)
Protecting Alabama
Protecting Fiona
Marrying Caroline (novella)
Protecting Summer
Protecting Cheyenne
Protecting Jessyka
Protecting Julie (novella)
Protecting Melody
Protecting the Future
Protecting Kiera (novella)
Protecting Alabama's Kids (novella)
Protecting Dakota

New York Times, *USA Today* and *Wall Street Journal* Bestselling Author Susan Stoker has a heart as big as the state of Tennessee where she lives, but this all American girl has also spent the last fourteen years living in Missouri, California, Colorado, Indiana, and Texas. She's married to a retired Army man who now gets to follow *her* around the country.

www.stokeraces.com
www.AcesPress.com
susan@stokeraces.com

Made in the USA
Coppell, TX
21 June 2023

18355993R00144